喚醒你的英文語感！

Get a Feel for English !

喚醒你的英文語感！

Get a Feel for English !

職場·托福·雅思·全民英檢 必備用書!

正確出口說英文

Properly Speaking in English

作者 — Dana Forsythe

APEX 高點登峰美語系列
Get education Group

Preface

All language learners should analyze themselves for error production. Language errors make our communication confusing, and they can make us seem unprofessional.

The most efficient way for Taiwanese to analyze themselves is to compare their English with errors that are commonly committed by Taiwanese people. By using this method, you can quickly begin to change your errors into correct production. Getting rid of errors means replacing errors with correct usage, so focusing on error correction is one of the fastest ways to improve language ability.

As you examine the errors in this book, you will notice some surprises, such as English that almost every Taiwanese person uses but that is incorrect, or even funny and confusing! If you get rid of these errors, you will push yourself to the top of the mountain of English users in Taiwan. Good luck.

Dana Forsythe

作者序

所有學習語言的人都應該分析自己製造出來的錯誤！語言文字上的錯誤會造成溝通上的困擾，更會使說話者的專業形象大打折扣。

最能幫助台灣學習者認清自己錯誤的方式就是，讓他們把自己的英文與台灣人常犯的錯誤做比較。透過這種方式，學習者能夠快速修正自己的錯誤。消弭錯誤就是以正確的用法取代以往的錯誤，因此，針對錯誤加以辨正，即是加強語言能力最快速的方法之一。

當你在檢視本書所列舉的錯誤時，會從中發覺一些令人驚訝的事，像是一些在台灣人人皆使用的英語，原來竟是不正確的，甚至是令人困惑的。只要你擺脫了本書所列舉的錯誤，你就能讓自己成為台灣英語使用者行列中的佼佼者！祝好運！

Dana Forsythe

編者序

要掌握一門語言，除了需要多聽多讀，更要多記、多用。但是在學習英文的過程中，有許多似是而非的觀念，如果觀念無法釐清，一直重複犯錯，不但會影響英語的學習，甚至會造成誤解。華人很容易受到中文思考邏輯習慣的影響，犯下一些典型的錯誤，本書針對國人最常犯的錯誤，逐一做有系統的介紹和解析，幫助讀者徹底釐清模糊的觀念，真正提升英文程度。

作者累積多年在台的豐富教學經驗，整理出最常見的英語錯誤用法，正誤並列，一眼即可洞察易錯的字詞。每一錯誤皆有完整清晰的說明解釋，深入淺出，使讀者了解造成錯誤的原因，幫助讀者釐清細微的文法語意錯誤，使英語能力更加精進。

本書將錯誤例句加以分類，目的在使學習者透過這些典型錯誤的分析，明白這些錯處在以英文為母語的人士眼中代表什麼意義，進而突破學習英文的障礙，掌握英文語法與語意的特質，培養使用正確英語的良好習慣。

本書使用說明

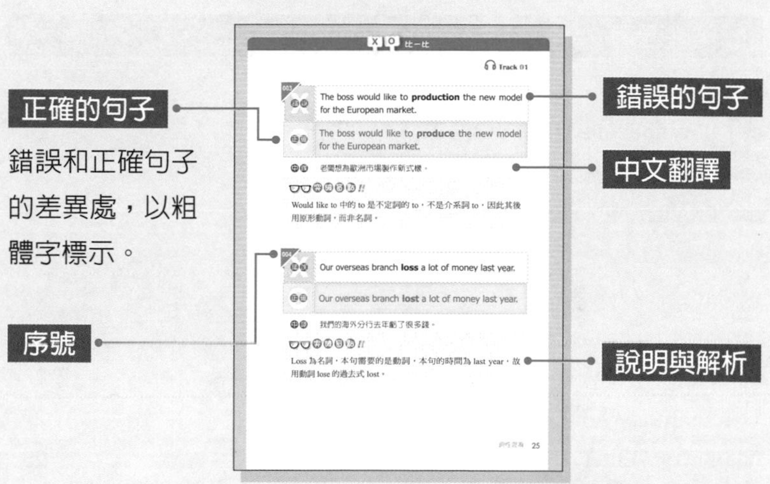

正確的句子

錯誤和正確句子的差異處，以粗體字標示。

MP3 播放曲目

每一首曲目會播放跨頁中呈現的四個句子。

例如：track 01 會播放序號 001~004 的句子。（僅少數曲目非 4 句）

只播放正確的英文句子，每個句子會重複一次。

CONTENTS

❖ 作者序 3　❖ 編者序 4　❖ 本書使用說明 5

1. 詞性混淆 Parts of Speech

a. VERBS

001 How spelling / How to spell 24
002 Product / Produce 24
003 Production / Produce 25
004 Loss / Lost 25
005 Advice / Advise 26
006 Adviced against / Advised against 26
007 Choice / Choose 27
008 Analysis / Analyze 27
009 Entry / Enter 28
010 Delivery / Deliver 28
011 Shop opens / Shop is open 29

b. NOUNS

012 Do you like here / Do you like this place 29
013 Confident / Confidence 30
014 Suggest / Suggestion 30
015 Economic / Economy 31
016 Demonstrate / Demonstration 31
017 Manufacture / Manufacturer 32
018 Good for your healthy / Good for your health 32
019 Brings lucky / Brings good luck 33

c. ADJECTIVES

020 Help / Helpful 33
021 Is finish / Is finished 34
022 Please / Pleased 34
023 Surprise / Surprised 35
024 Economy / Economical 35
025 Detail / Detailed 36
026 Disappointment / Disappointed 36
027 Advance / Advanced 37
028 Fashion / Fashionable 37
029 Trustable / Trustworthy 38
030 He was died / He was dead 38

d. NATION and NATIONALITY

031 British / Britain 39
032 Korea / Korean 39

2. 動詞 Verbs

A. 錯選動詞 Verb Choice Errors

033 I'll go first / I'm leaving now 42
034 There happened a fire / There was a fire 42
035 They have a lot of people / There are a lot of people 43
036 Sorry I came late / Sorry I am late 43
037 Is anyone have / Does anyone have 44
038 Are you agree / Do you agree 44
039 So am I / So do I 45
040 Go play after work / Go have some fun after work 45
041 Make the party / Have the party 46

042 Spent a good time with you / Had a good time with you 46
043 Join the entrance exam / Take the entrance exam 47
044 Eating Chinese medicine / Taking Chinese medicine 47
045 Spend a long time / Take a long time 48
046 Cost you two hours / Take you two hours 48
047 Talks about / Is about 49
048 Concerns about / Is about 49
049 May I have a question / May I ask a question 50
050 Could you like to wait / Would you like to wait 50
051 I'm finding / I'm trying to find 51
052 When did you know / When did you find out 51
053 Borrow me a pencil / Lend (Loan) me a pencil 52
054 Do a sightseeing / Go sightseeing 52
055 Let you feel relaxed / Make you feel relaxed 53
056 Nice to meet you / Nice to see you 53
057 Have you ever met a typhoon / Have you ever experienced a typhoon 54
058 Joined college / Entered college 54
059 Lived at the hotel / Stayed at the hotel 55
060 Down the price / Lower the price 55
061 Company was built / Company was established 56
062 Cancel the presentation until / Postpone the presentation until 56
063 Open the stereo / Turn on the stereo 57
064 Seeing interesting programs / Watching interesting programs 57
065 Rise the screen / Raise the screen 58
066 Win / Beat 58
067 He has out / He has gone out 59
068 Learned knowledge / Gained knowledge 59
069 I hope I could / I wish I could 60

070 I like to make an appointment / I would like to make an appointment 60

B. 動詞形式的錯誤 Verb Form Errors

a. IRREGULAR VERBS

071 Buyed / Bought 61
072 We've selled out / We've sold out 61
073 Got stucked / Got stuck 62

b. AGREEMENT

074 My company always expect / My company always expects 62
075 A lot of potential customers is / A lot of potential customers are 63
076 What is the advantages / What are the advantages 63
077 Everybody ... were very happy / Everybody ... was very happy 64
078 The shipment of T-shirts were / The shipment of T-shirts was 64
079 your ... software work great / your ... software works great 65
080 Do your product / Does your product 65

c. INFINITIVES

081 Forced him accept / Forced him to accept 66
082 Could you manage repairing it / Could you manage to repair it 66
083 Allow me to introducing myself / Allow me to introduce myself 67
084 Decided going alone / Decided to go alone 67
085 It will be our pleasure treating you / It will be our pleasure to treat you 68
086 Nice meet you / Nice to meet you 68

d. ACTIVE / PASSIVE

087 I was majored in / I majored in 69
088 My arm is hurt when / My arm hurts when 69

089 Will you promote to her position / Will you be promoted to her position 70
090 [It] can use to / [It] can be used to 70
091 Candidates were select by / Candidates were selected by 71
092 The report was sending to / The report was sent to 71
093 Were borned in England / Were born in England 72

e. PARTICIPLES

094 I am call to talk to / I am calling to talk to 72
095 Look forward to see it / Look forward to seeing it 73
096 Is relating to / Is related to 73
097 Hear the train to come / Hear the train coming 74
098 Want to go to bowling / Want to go bowling 74

f. UNNECESSARY VERBS

099 Is no longer exist / No longer exists 75
100 I am like / I like 75
101 We are agree / We agree 76
102 It is work now / It works now 76
103 Is save time / Saves time 77
104 Everything I can do to / Everything I can do 77

g. MISSING/INCOMPLETE VERBS

105 Let's back to / Let's go back to 78
106 And no focus / And has no focus 78
107 What time will you sleep tonight / What time will you go to sleep tonight 79
108 Don't concern / Don't be concerned 79
109 When I back to Taiwan / When I go back to Taiwan 80

h. OTHER

110 Let you to replace / Let you replace 80

111 She made us to leave / She made us leave 81

112 I ever learned piano / I learned piano 81

113 I have ever been to / I've been to 82

114 Marry with a Taiwanese woman / Marry a Taiwanese woman 82

115 Come for having dinner / Come to have dinner / Come for dinner 83

116 Rather to go camping / Rather go camping 83

117 I suggest that you to try / I suggest that you try 84

118 Recommended that we placed / Recommended that we place 84

119 You can setting the temperature / You can set the temperature 85

120 I should to be free / I should be free 85

121 Take turn / Take turns 86

122 Welcome you to / We welcome you to / Welcome to 86

123 If we offer ... they would / If we offer ... they will / If we offered ... they would 87

124 Lack of confidence / Lacks confidence 87

125 Determines to be the manager / Is determined to be the manager 88

C. 動詞時態的錯誤 Verb Tense Errors

a. PRESENT TIME

126 Is including / Includes 88

127 We didn't produce [those] / We don't produce [those] 89

128 As you could see / As you can see 89

129 I had learned many things / I have learned many things 90

130 Have you ever get / Have you ever got 90

131 I am ... for one year / I have been ... for one year 91

132 I divide my presentation / I have divided my presentation 91

133 We have improve our product / We have improved our product 92

134 We are in the shoe business since / We've been in the shoe business since 92
135 Is always well-known / Has always been well-known 93
136 Recently we are working on / Recently we've been working on 94
137 I am studying English since / I've been studying English since 94

b. PAST TIME

138 I had placed the order last week / I placed the order last week 95
139 Had sent a letter yesterday / Sent a letter yesterday 95
140 We have invested a lot / We invested a lot 96
141 He almost go crazy / He almost went crazy 96
142 Did nothing but watched / Did nothing but watch 97
143 I was having a headache / I had a headache 97
144 Do you have lunch yet / Did you have lunch yet 98
145 When did they told you / When did they tell you 98
146 If I had the money / If I had had the money 99
147 I was used to worry / I used to worry 99
148 Finish what I was say / Finish what I was saying 100
149 We didn't went / We didn't go 100
150 Must stay up / Had to stay up 101
151 He was died / He died 101

c. FUTURE TIME

152 What happen / What will happen 102
153 After they will sign the contract / After they sign the contract 102

D. 片語動詞 Phrasal Verbs

a. PARTICLE ERRORS

154 Pay more attention on / Pay more attention to 103

155 Made by / Made of 103
156 Pick up / Pick out 104
157 Concerned with / Concerned about 104
158 Inferior than / Inferior to 105
159 Open it by / Open it with 105

b. TRANSITIVE VERBS

160 Consider about our offer / Consider our offer 106
161 Discuss about / Discuss 106
162 Mention about / Mention 107
163 Stress on the importance / Stress the importance 107
164 Emphasize on the need / Emphasize the need 108
165 Contact with you / Contact you 108
166 Accompanied with me / Accompanied me 109
167 Requests for / Requests 109
168 Write down / Write it down 110
169 Do you like / Do you like it 110
170 Introduce to / Introduce it to 111

c. INTRANSITIVE VERBS

171 Participate the trade show / Participate in the trade show 111
172 Don't laugh me / Don't laugh at me 112
173 Waiting your response / Waiting for your response 112
174 Waiting me for thirty minutes / Waiting for me for thirty minutes 113
175 Like listening music / Like listening to music 113

d. VERBS USED WITH PREPOSITIONS

176 Prepare the negotiation / Prepare for the negotiation 114

177 Comment your suggestion / Comment on your suggestion 114
178 Insist the cooperation / Insist on the cooperation 115
179 Complains the long hours / Complains about the long hours 115
180 Objects Helen's ideas / Objects to Helen's ideas 116
181 Apply a new job / Apply for a new job 116
182 Don't worry it / Don't worry about it 117
183 I explained to you / I explained it to you 117
184 Search the solution / Search for the solution 118
185 Agree me / Agree with me 118

e. IDIOMATIC PHRASAL VERBS

186 Pay attention what / Pay attention to what 119
187 Enter an agreement / Enter into an agreement 119
188 Focus / Focus on 120
189 Try some new clothes / Try on some new clothes 120
190 Find out some information / Find some information 121

3. 名詞 Nouns

A. 錯選名詞 Noun Choice Errors

191 Effect / Effectiveness 124
192 Bus fee / Bus fare 124
193 I have no power / I have no energy 125
194 Pay a fee to use the highway / Pay a toll to use the highway 125
195 Clients / Customers 126
196 Father / Priest 126
197 The chairs are too small / The seats are too small 127
198 Learned subjects / Learned things / Studied subjects 127
199 Free of cost / Free of charge 128

B. 名詞形式的錯誤 Noun Form Errors

200 Good cooker / Good cook 128

201 I see you mean / I see your meaning / I see what you mean 129

202 Your meaning / You mean 129

203 No air condition / No air conditioner / No air conditioning 130

204 Want something special price / Want a special price / Want something at a special price 130

C. 數量與複數 Number / Plurals

205 Point / Points 131

206 Followings are / Following are 131

207 Sales figure / Sales figures 132

208 Salespeople / Salesperson 132

209 One hundred peoples / One hundred people 133

210 I am Taiwanese people / I am a Taiwanese person 133

211 I have three childs / I have three children 134

212 Every customers like / Every customer likes 134

D. 可數與不可數 Countable/Uncountable

213 Many hard works / Much hard work 135

214 Advices / Advice 135

215 Good advices / Good advice 136

216 Conduct a market research / Conduct market research 136

217 In my professional views / In my professional view 137

218 Many evidences / A lot of evidence 137

219 Furnitures / Furniture 138

220 A good news / Good news / Some good news 138

221 A good news / Some good news 139

222 Equipments / Equipment 139
223 Mails / Mail 140
224 Staffs / Staff 140
225 Characters / Character 141
226 Caused a lot of damages / Caused a lot of damage 141
227 A hard work / Hard work 142
228 A glue / Some glue 142
229 An important information / An important piece of information 143
230 Have a lunch together / Have lunch together 143

E. 限定詞 Determiners

231 Close door / Close the door 144
232 Inquire about laser printer / Inquire about the laser printer 144
233 Attend meeting / Attend the meeting 145
234 What is difference / What is the difference 146
235 Most of factory workers / Most of the factory workers 146
236 Read all of instructions / Read all of the instructions 147

F. 代名詞 Pronouns

237 He is our sales agent / This is our sales agent 147
238 Relax yourself / Relax 148
239 If you are convenient / if it is convenient 148
240 Here is Taiwan / This is Taiwan 149
241 A friend of him / A friend of his 149

G. 動名詞 Gerunds

242 Delay to ship / Delay shipping 150
243 Open by push / Open by pushing 150

244 Before turn on / Before turning on 151
245 Risk to promote / Risk promoting 151
246 Look forward to hear / Look forward to hearing 152
247 Mind to explain / Mind explaining 152
248 Avoid to miss / Avoid missing 153
249 Enjoy to talk / Enjoy talking 153
250 Do you remember to cancel / Do you remember canceling / Did you remember to cancel 154
251 For come / For coming 154
252 Enjoy to walk / Enjoy walking 155
253 Stop to say that / Stop saying that 155
254 It's worth to see / It's worth seeing 156
255 Used to eat / Used to eating 156
256 In addition to give / In addition to giving 157
257 Due to Maggie forgot / Due to Maggie's forgetting 157
258 After finish / After I finish / After finishing 158
259 Thanks for your calling / Thanks for calling / Thanks for your call 158
260 Run a meeting / Running a meeting / To run a meeting 159

H. 子句 Clauses

261 No matter they propose / No matter what they propose 159
262 The reason is because / The reason is that 160
263 Need to be resolved / That need to be resolved 160

4. 形容詞 Adjectives

264 We are very interesting / We are very interested 162
265 Feel so boring / Feel so bored 162
266 More cheaper / cheaper 163

267 I'm not clear / I'm not clear about 163

268 More discount / A larger discount 164

269 Your another model / another model / other models 164

270 The another restaurant / Another restaurant 165

271 Less happier / Less happy 165

272 A twelve hours flight / A twelve-hour flight 166

273 A childhood of carefree / A carefree childhood 166

274 Ashame of yourself / Ashamed of yourself 167

275 There is no any reason / There is no reason / There is not any reason 167

276 I a little afraid / I am a little afraid 168

277 I don't busy / I'm not busy 168

278 Today was too tired/Today was too tiring/Today I was too tired 169

279 Shoes store / Shoe store 169

280 A big and black coat / A big black coat 170

281 [It] was too disgusted / [It] was too disgusting 171

282 North Taiwan / Northern Taiwan 171

283 Tea is too thick / Tea is too strong 172

284 The [X] are not enough / There are not enough [X] 172

285 A funny place / A fun place 173

286 All the flight / The whole flight 173

287 Mistaking / Mistaken 174

288 You are so poor! / Poor you! 174

289 On sale / For sale 175

290 Things are well / Things are good 175

5. 副詞 Adverbs

291 Easy to become angry / Becomes angry easily / Easily becomes angry 178

292 Very like / Like very much 178

293 Very like / Like very much 179
294 For three times / Three times 179
295 Quickly / Right away 180
296 In last month / Last month 180
297 Recently questions / Recently 181
298 I love there / I love it there 181
299 Almost come from / Almost all come from 182
300 Is much desirable / Is much more desirable 182
301 For five times / Five times 183
302 At there / There 183

6. 介系詞 Prepositions

A. 表時間的介系詞 Prepositions of Time

303 At the mornings / In the mornings 186
304 Work at the evening / Work in the evening 186
305 In the night / At night 187
306 Call during 8 to 5 / Call from 8 to 5 187
307 At New Year's Day / On New Year's Day 188
308 On May / In May 188
309 Since three weeks / For three weeks 189
310 Started to produce [X] since 1995 / Has been producing [X] since 1995 / Started producing [X] in 1995 189
311 Went ... during two days / Went ... for two days 190

B. 表位置的介系詞 Prepositions of Place

312 Arrives Los Angeles / Arrives in Los Angeles 190
313 In the second floor / On the second floor 191
314 On mainland China / In mainland China 191

315 Put on the letter / Put in the letter 192
316 At the website / On the website 192
317 Put details on report / Put details in report 193
318 Arrive to the airport / Arrive at the airport 193
319 Stayed in home / Stayed at home 194
320 In the right side of the road / On the right side of the road 194
321 Stayed on bed / Stayed in bed 195
322 Studying in the university / Studying at the university 195
323 Nearby / Near 196

C. 其他介系詞 Other Prepositions

324 Difficult to me / Difficult for me 196
325 The reason of your complaint / The reason for your complaint 197
326 Divided by two main divisions / Divided into two main divisions 197
327 Heard the news through the radio / Heard the news on the radio 198
328 According to my opinion / In my opinion 198
329 The answer of the question / The answer to the question 199
330 Not very good in English / Not very good at English 199
331 Say you / Say to you / Tell you 200
332 What did you tell to her / What did you tell her 200
333 Mention about it / Mention it 201

7. 疑問句 Questions

A. 直接和間接問句 Direct and Indirect Questions

334 How to spell it / How do you spell it 204
335 How to pronounce / How do you pronounce 204
336 How to say that / How do you say that 205

337 How it can be used / How can it be used 205
338 Could you tell me where can I find / Could you tell me where I can find 206

B. 其他問句 Other Questions

339 Are you come to visit / Are you coming to visit / Will you come to visit 206
340 Are you study Chinese / Do you study Chinese / Are you studying Chinese 207
341 Do you still thirsty / Are you still thirsty 207
342 Do you like to attend / Do you want to attend / Would you like to attend 208
343 Would you like watching / Would you like to watch 208
344 What we can do / What can we do 209
345 What is the difference of / What is the difference between 209
346 How should I do / What should I do 210
347 How do you think / What do you think? 210
348 How about your weekend / How was your weekend 211

8. 其他錯誤 Other Errors

A. 否定表達 Negatives / Negation

349 Neither coffee or tea / Neither coffee nor tea 214
350 Can not hardly wait / Can hardly wait 214
351 I don't think ..., too / I don't think ..., either 215
352 Sounds not good / Doesn't sound good 215

B. 話語標記 Discourse Markers

353 Besides / Besides that 216
354 Although ... but / Although / but 217
355 Since ... so / Since ... / ... so 218
356 At last / Last / Finally 218

357 At first / First 219
358 As I know / As far as I know 220

C. 時間表達 Time

359 For two years / Two years ago 220
360 One week two times / Two times a week / Twice a week 221
361 Older than me five years / Five years older than me 221
362 Last time when / Last time 222
363 At midnight / In the middle of the night 222
364 I saw her five years before / I saw her five years ago 223
365 What time / When 223
366 Arrive ten minutes later / Arrive in ten minutes 224

D. 文字順序 Word Order (Inversions)

367 Here Joe comes / Here comes Joe 224
368 Eastsouth / Southeast 225
369 Left lower / Lower left 225
370 Filled in it / Filled it in 226
371 Take apart it / Take it apart 226
372 How expensive is their product / How expensive their product is 227
373 The responsible person / The person responsible 227
374 Two my ideas / my two ideas 228

1

詞性混淆
Parts of Speech

a. VERBS

001

A: Can you tell me the name of their company again?

錯誤 B: Yeah, but I don't know **how spelling**.

正確 B: Yeah, but I don't know **how to spell it**.

中譯 A：你可不可以再跟我說一次他們公司的名字？
B：好，但是我不知道怎麼拼。

突破盲點!!

Spelling 是（動）名詞，在疑問詞 how 之後應使用不定詞，即，to V。

002

錯誤 We **product** OEM parts.

正確 We **produce** OEM parts.

中譯 我們代工生產零件。

突破盲點!!

Product 為名詞，本句需要的是動詞，故改為 produce。（OEM 為 original equipment manufacturer 之省略）

Track 01

003 錯誤

The boss would like to **production** the new model for the European market.

正確

The boss would like to **produce** the new model for the European market.

中譯 老闆想為歐洲市場製作新式樣。

突破盲點!!

Would like to 中的 to 是不定詞的 to，不是介系詞 to，因此其後用原形動詞，而非名詞。

004 錯誤

Our overseas branch **loss** a lot of money last year.

正確

Our overseas branch **lost** a lot of money last year.

中譯 我們的海外分行去年虧了很多錢。

突破盲點!!

Loss 為名詞，本句需要的是動詞，本句的時間為 last year，故用動詞 lose 的過去式 lost。

005

錯誤 Please **advice** us of how to handle the shipping.

正確 Please **advise** us of how to handle the shipping.

中譯 請建議我們怎樣處理貨運事宜。

Advice 為名詞，advise 才是動詞，不可混淆；本句需要的是動詞 advise。

006

錯誤 The lawyer **adviced against** signing the contract.

正確 The lawyer **advised against** signing the contract.

中譯 律師勸我不要簽合約。

Advice 是名詞（無過去式），advise 為動詞；本句需要的是動詞，故改為 advised。

Track 02

007 錯誤 You can **choice** black or silver.

正確 You can **choose** black or silver.

中譯 你可以選擇黑色或銀色的。

突破盲點!!

原句中助動詞 can 應接（原形）動詞，choice 為名詞，應改為 choose。

008 錯誤 Can you **analysis** the product specifications again?

正確 Can you **analyze** the product specifications again?

中譯 你可以把產品規格再分析一次嗎？

突破盲點!!

Analysis 為名詞，而本句中需要的是動詞，故改為 analyze。

009 錯誤 You need an access card to **entry** the office.

正確 You need an access card to **enter** the office.

中譯 你需要一張通行卡才能進入辦公室。

本句中的 to 為不定詞的 to，而非介系詞，其後應跟原形動詞，故將 entry 改為 enter。

010 錯誤 You will **delivery** the drinks each week, right?

正確 You will **deliver** the drinks each week, right?

中譯 你會每個星期運送飲料，對嗎？

原句中的 delivery 為一名詞，因其前為助動詞 will，故知應改為動詞 deliver。

Track 03

011

錯誤 Our shop **opens** every day from 9 a.m. to 6 p.m.

正確 Our shop **is open** every day from 9 a.m. to 6 p.m.

中譯 我們的店每天早上九點營業到下午六點。

突破盲點!!

動詞 open 指開的「動作」，本句應選用形容詞的 open 表示開的「狀態」。

b. NOUNS

012

A: This is my first time to eat at a real Chinese restaurant.

錯誤 B: Oh. Do you like **here**?

正確 B: Oh. Do you like **this place**?

中譯 A：這是我第一次在真正的中國餐廳吃飯。
B：噢，你喜歡這個地方嗎？

突破盲點!!

Here 雖是「這裡」的意思，但是它是副詞，不可當受詞，應改為 this place。

013 錯誤

Our editing team has a lot of **confident** in our travel books.

正確

Our editing team has a lot of **confidence** in our travel books.

中譯　我們的編輯小組對我們的旅遊書籍很有信心。

突破盲點!!

在 a lot of 後接名詞（可數、不可數皆可），而 confident 為形容詞，故改為 confidence。

014 錯誤

My **suggest** is that we buy fifty units.

正確

My **suggestion** is that we buy fifty units.

中譯　我的建議是我們買五十個。

突破盲點!!

My 為第一人稱代名詞所有格，其後應接其所有之名詞，而 suggest 為動詞，故應改為 suggestion。

Track 04

015

錯誤 Many people are concerned about the **economic**.

正確 Many people are concerned about the **economy**.

中譯 許多人擔心經濟。

突破盲點!!

Economic 是形容詞，economy 是名詞，原句中因其前有定冠詞，故應用名詞。

016

錯誤 Our sales staff can give you a **demonstrate** of the tools.

正確 Our sales staff can give you a **demonstration** of the tools.

中譯 我們的銷售人員可以為你示範說明如何使用工具。

突破盲點!!

Give 為一授與動詞，其後除間接受詞（一般是「人」外），再接直接受詞（一般是「物」），故將動詞 demonstrate 改為名詞，作 give 的直接受詞。

017

錯誤 Now we use a **manufacture** in Singapore.

正確 Now we use a **manufacturer** in Singapore.

中譯 現在我們用新加坡的製造商。

突破盲點!!

Manufacture「製造」為動詞，因其前已有動詞，並有不定冠詞 a，故知應改為名詞 manufacturer「製造商」。

018

錯誤 Chinese tea is good for your **healthy**.

正確 1. Chinese tea is good for your **health**.

正確 2. Chinese tea is good for you.

中譯 中國茶有益健康。

突破盲點!!

Healthy 是形容詞，本句需要的是名詞 health。此外，"Good for you" 的說法比 "good for your health." 更為普遍。

Track 05

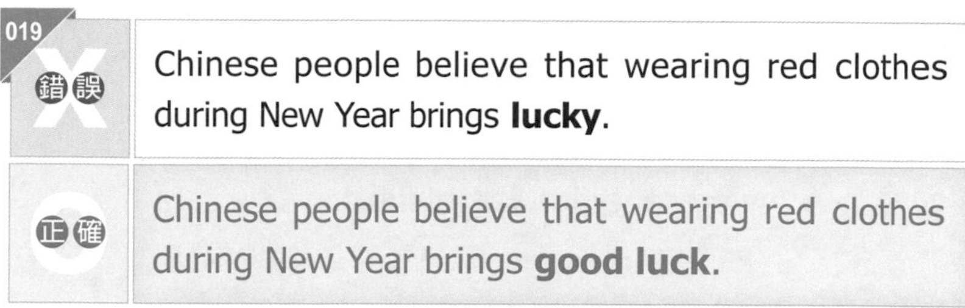

019

錯誤 Chinese people believe that wearing red clothes during New Year brings **lucky**.

正確 Chinese people believe that wearing red clothes during New Year brings **good luck**.

中譯　中國人相信在新年穿紅衣服會帶來好運。

突破盲點!!

Lucky 為形容詞，本句需要名詞 luck 作動詞 bring 的受詞，而 luck 的意思是「運氣」，因要表「好」運，故加形容詞 good 修飾 luck。

c. ADJECTIVES

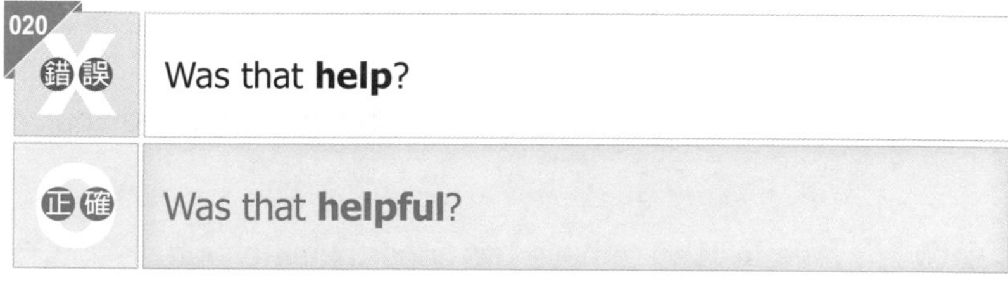

020

錯誤 Was that **help**?

正確 Was that **helpful**?

中譯　那樣有幫助嗎？

突破盲點!!

Help 為動詞或名詞，若是前者則本句不合文法，若為後者則語意不明，因此改為形容詞 helpful。

021

錯誤 My presentation is finish.

正確 1. My presentation is **finished**.

正確 2. My presentation is **over**.

正確 3. My presentation is **done**.

中譯 1. 我的簡報做完了。2. 我的簡報結束了。3. 我的簡報做好了。

突破盲點!!

Finish 為動詞，其過去分詞 finished 則可作形容詞，意思就是 over「完畢」、done「完成」。

022

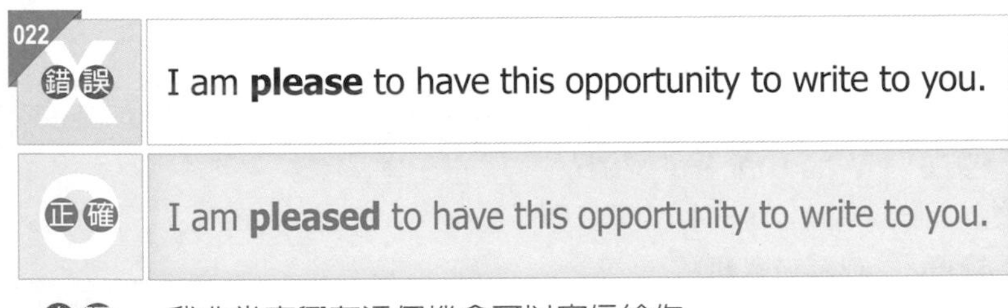

錯誤 I am **please** to have this opportunity to write to you.

正確 I am **pleased** to have this opportunity to write to you.

中譯 我非常高興有這個機會可以寫信給你。

突破盲點!!

注意本句中的 please 不是「請」（副詞）的意思和用法；please 可作動詞用，意思是「使……高興」，而本句則應用 pleased，即由 please 的過去分詞轉用的形容詞，意思為「高興的」。

Track 06

023

錯誤 You seem **surprise** to hear the news.

正確 You seem **surprised** to hear the news.

中譯 你聽到這個消息好像很驚訝。

突破盲點!!

Seem 為一連綴動詞，其後應接形容詞，作為主詞補語；而 surprised 為過去分詞轉用之形容詞。

024

錯誤 The larger package is more **economy**.

正確 The larger package is more **economical**.

中譯 較大的包裝比較經濟。

突破盲點!!

本句中的 more 為「更」(副詞)，而非「較多」(形容詞)的意思，其後應為形容詞 economical，而非名詞 economy。

025 錯誤 Your report is very **detail**.

正確 Your report is very **detailed**.

中譯 你的報告非常詳盡。

Detail 作名詞意思為「細節」，作動詞意思為「詳述」，在 very 後本句需要的應是形容詞，故改為 detailed「詳盡的」(過去分詞轉形容詞)。

026 錯誤 I am a bit **disappointment** with the quality of their work.

正確 I am a bit **disappointed** with the quality of their work.

中譯 我對他們的工作品質有點失望。

本句中的 a bit 為副詞，其後應為被其修飾的對象，即形容詞 disappointed。

Track 07

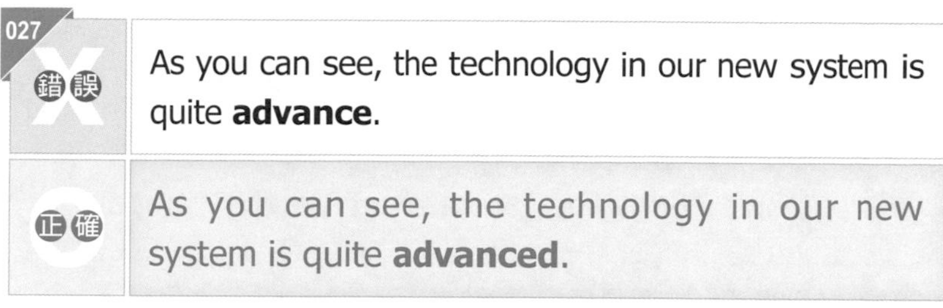

中譯　如你所見，我們新系統的技術相當先進。

突破盲點!!

Quite 為副詞，應用來修飾形容詞，而 advanced 為過去分詞轉用的形容詞。

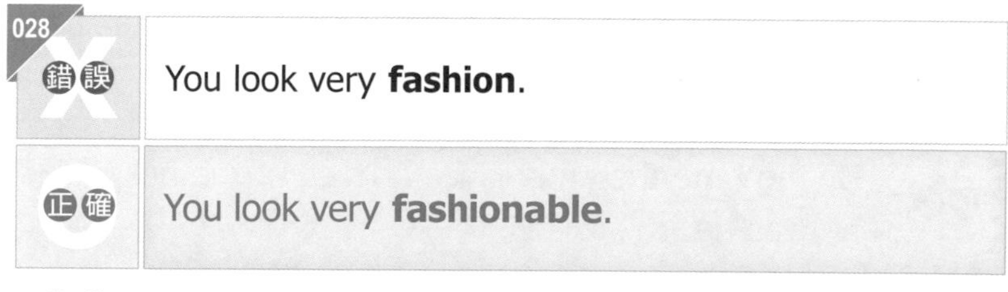

中譯　你很時髦。

突破盲點!!

Fashion 為名詞，其形容詞為 fashionable，不應混淆。

029 錯誤

Don't worry. They are a **trustable** company.

正確

Don't worry. They are a **trustworthy** company.

中譯　別擔心。他們是值得信賴的公司。

突破盲點!!

Trustable 較 trustworthy 不正式，雖有人用，但有些字典卻未納入，為了避免不必要的爭議以選用 trustworthy 為佳。

030 錯誤

By the time the ambulance arrived at the hospital, he was **died**.

正確

By the time the ambulance arrived at the hospital, he was **dead**.

中譯　當救護車到達醫院的同時，他已過世了。

突破盲點!!

Died 為動詞 die 的過去式，不可與形容詞 dead 混淆。

Track 08

d. NATION and NATIONALITY

031

錯誤 Did you ship the crates to **British** yet?

正確 Did you ship the crates to **Britain** yet?

中譯 板條箱你運送到英國了嗎？

突破盲點!!

British 為形容詞，Britain「不列顛」才是名詞。(「大不列顛」為 Great Britain。)

032

錯誤 The two leaders in this field are **Korean** and Japan.

正確 The two leaders in this field are **Korea** and Japan.

中譯 這個領域的兩個先驅是韓國和日本。

突破盲點!!

本句之主詞 leaders 並非指「人」，而是指「國家」，故將 Korean 改為 Korea。另，注意對等連接詞 and 所連接的應是對等的兩個名詞，即「韓國」與「日本」。

NOTES

2

動詞
Verbs

A. 錯選動詞 Verb Choice Errors

B. 動詞形式的錯誤 Verb Form Errors

C. 動詞時態的錯誤 Verb Tense Errors

D. 片語動詞 Phrasal Verbs

A. 錯選動詞 Verb Choice Errors

(Two people are in the office at the end of the day.)

033

錯誤 A: I will **go** first.

正確 A: I'm **leaving** now.

B: Okay. See you tomorrow.

中譯 （一天結束時，兩個人在辦公室裡。）
A：我先走囉！ B：好，明天見。

突破盲點!!

Go 原則上為「去」的意思，本句表達的則為「離開」之意，故應使用 leave。

034

錯誤 **There happened a fire** in the warehouse last night.

正確 **There was a fire** in the warehouse last night.

中譯 昨晚倉庫發生了一場火災。

突破盲點!!

There + be 是「有」的意思（there 視為虛主詞），為固定用法；happen 為一普通動詞，不以 there 為主詞。

Track 09

035 錯誤 **There have** a lot of people on this street.

正確 **There are** a lot of people on this street.

中譯　這條街上有很多人。

There + be 是「有」的意思，表示在某處有某人、事、物的存在； there 為一虛主詞，真正主詞為 be 動詞後的名詞。

036 錯誤 Sorry I **came** late. The traffic is terrible today.

正確 Sorry I **am** late. The traffic is terrible today.

中譯　對不起我遲到了。今天交通堵塞。

突破盲點!!

Came 為 come 的過去式，讓人覺得是在說過去（比如，昨天）發生的事；一般講「遲到」，用 be 動詞即可。

037

錯誤 **Is** anyone have any questions?

正確 **Does** anyone have any questions?

中譯　有人有任何問題嗎？

Have 在本句中作普通動詞用，故構成問句時需用助動詞 does，而非 be 動詞 is。

038

錯誤 **Are** you agree with me?

正確 **Do** you agree with me?

中譯　你贊同我嗎？

Agree 為一普通動詞，要構成疑問句須用助動詞 do，而非 be 動詞。

Track 10

039

A: I feel so happy today.

錯誤 B: So **am** I.

正確 B: So **do** I.

中譯 A：我今天覺得好開心。
B：我也是。

突破盲點!!

上列對話中，A 說他 feel「覺得」很開心，因此 B 說的「我也是」應指他也「覺得」開心，故應用助動詞 do 來代替 feel。

040

錯誤 Do you want to go **play** after work?

正確 Do you want to go **have some fun** after work?

中譯 你下班後要娛樂一下嗎？

突破盲點!!

Play 指「玩耍」或「玩遊戲」，不適用本句；本句應採 have some fun「找點樂子、輕鬆一下」。

041

A: Where will the party be?

錯誤 B: We'll **make** the party at my place.

正確 B: We'll **have** the party at my place.

中譯 A：派對會在哪裡呢？

B：我們會在我家開派對。

突破盲點!!

「開派對」英文叫 have a party，不是 make a party。

042

錯誤 I **spent** a good time with you last night.

正確 I **had** a good time with you last night.

中譯 我昨晚和你玩得很愉快。

突破盲點!!

Spend 指「用」或「花」時間，其後跟「一般時間」，如：I spent two hours reading the report.；「玩得愉快」應用 have a good time 表示。

Track 11

043

錯誤 I'll **join** the entrance exam next weekend.

正確 I'll **take** the entrance exam next weekend.

中譯 我下週末要考入學考試。

突破盲點!!

Join 通常指「參加機構、組織或團體」；參加考試的「參加」應用 take。

044

錯誤 If you have a cold, try **eating** some Chinese medicine.

正確 If you have a cold, try **taking** some Chinese medicine.

中譯 如果你感冒了，試試吃些中藥。

突破盲點!!

「吃藥」英文用 take medicine，而不用 eat medicine；eat 的受詞通常為「食物類」，如：eat a hamburger，而 take 則用在「藥品類」之前，如：take vitamins。

Did **you spend** a long time to get here?

正確 Did **it take (you)** a long time to get here?

中譯 你花了很久的時間來這裡嗎？

Spend time Ving 指「（人）花時間做某事」，如：I spent two hours cooking.；sth. take (sb.) time to V 則指「（事）花（人）時間去做」。

It will **cost** you about two hours to drive there.

正確 It will **take** you about two hours to drive there.

中譯 你大概會花兩個小時開車到那兒。

突破盲點!!

Cost 指「花錢」，如：It cost me $10.；「花時間」應該用 take。注意，若主詞為「人」，則動詞都用 spend。

Track 12

047 錯誤

This book **talks about/is talking** the ten principles of business success.

正確

This book **is about** the ten principles of business success.

中譯　這本書是關於企業成功的十項準則。

突破盲點!!

本句主詞為 this book，是無生命的「事物」，故不應用帶「動作」的動詞 talk，應選用不帶動作的連綴動詞 be。

048 錯誤

The memo **concerns about** the recent absentee problem.

正確

1. The memo **is about** the recent absentee problem.

正確

2. The memo **concerns** the recent absentee problem.

中譯　備忘錄是有關最近缺席者的問題。

突破盲點!!

Concern「與……有關」為一及物動詞，其後不須介系詞 about（勿與片語 be concerned about 混淆）；本句亦可用 be 動詞後接介系詞 about 表達「關於」。

049

錯誤 May I **have** a question?

正確 May I **ask** a question?

中譯 我可以問問題嗎？

突破盲點!!

Have a question 是「有問題」的意思；「問問題」應用 ask a question。

050

錯誤 **Could** you like to wait for her?

正確 **Would** you like to wait for her?

中譯 你想等她嗎？

突破盲點!!

Would you like to ... ? 的意思是「你想要……嗎？」是固定用法，不可任意更改。

Track 13

051

錯誤

Can you wait for me a moment?
I am **finding** my wallet.

正確

Can you wait for me a moment?
I am **trying to find** my wallet.

中譯　你可以等我一下嗎？我在試著找我的皮夾。

突破盲點!!

Find 的意思是「找到」，就其語意而言不應使用進行式。（如果指「正在找」，可以說 I'm looking for ...。）

052

錯誤

When did you **know** the new manager is Tom?

正確

When did you **find out** the new manager is Tom?

中譯　你何時發現新經理是湯姆？

突破盲點!!

Know 指「知道、認識」的「狀態」，如：I know Dr. Johnson very well.；而本句問的是「發現」這個「動作」所發生的時間，故不用 know，而用 find out。

Can you **borrow** me a pencil?

Can you **lend/loan** me a pencil?

中譯　你可以借我一支筆嗎？

Borrow 指「借入」，如：Can I borrow your pen?，而 lend 或 loan 則指「借出」。

Do you want to **do a** sightseeing with us?

Do you want to **go** sightseeing with us?

中譯　你想和我們去觀光嗎？

「觀光」英文要說 go sightseeing，沒有 do a sightseeing 的用法。

Track 14

055

錯誤 Have a drink after work. It will **let** you feel relaxed.

正確 Have a drink after work. It will **make** you feel relaxed.

中譯 下班後去喝一杯吧。這樣可以使你放輕鬆。

突破盲點!!

Let 和 make 都可作使役動詞；但前者是「讓」的意思，主詞通常是「人」，而後者則為「使」，主詞並無特別限制。

056

(Two friends see each other at a restaurant.)

錯誤 A: Henry, nice to **meet** you!

正確 A: Henry, nice to **see** you!

中譯 （兩個朋友在餐廳遇見。）
A：亨利，真高興見到你！

突破盲點!!

Nice to meet you. 用於「（經介紹）初認識人時」；「已經認識，再次見面時」應說 Nice to see you.，不然對方會以為你忘記他了！

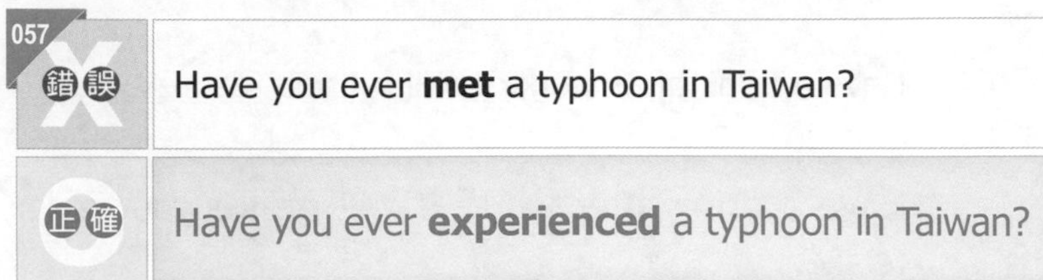

中譯　你在台灣有遇過颱風嗎？

突破盲點!!

Meet 一般指「與人相遇或認識」；「碰到或遇到某種狀況（如天氣）」則應用 experience「經歷」。

058

錯誤　I **joined** college when I was just seventeen.

正確　I **entered** college when I was just seventeen.

中譯　我進大學時才十七歲。

突破盲點!!

「進大學」用 enter college 即可，不可說成 join college。（但注意，「入伍、從軍」是 join the army，不可說成 enter the army。）

Track 15

059

錯誤 We **lived** at the hotel for three nights.

正確 We **stayed** at the hotel for three nights.

中譯 我們在這間旅館住宿 3 個晚上。

突破盲點!!

「短暫的居住」英文要用 stay，不可用 live；live 指「長期的居住」。

060

錯誤 Can you **down** the price?

正確 Can you **lower/reduce/cut** the price?

中譯 你可以降低／減少／削減價錢嗎？

突破盲點!!

本句的第一個字為助動詞，故句中須有一「主動詞」，而 down 並非動詞而是副詞，故應將其改為 lower、reduce 或 cut。

061 錯誤 My company was **built** in 1995.

正確 1. My company was **established** in 1995.

正確 2. My company was **founded** in 1995.

中譯 1. 我的公司在一九九五年創立。
2. 我的公司在一九九五年建立。

突破盲點!!

Build 通常指「建造」，本句的主詞為「公司」，並非「建築物」，因此動詞應用 establish 或 found。

062 錯誤 I'm afraid I have to **cancel** the presentation until tomorrow.

正確 I'm afraid I have to **postpone** the presentation until tomorrow.

中譯 我恐怕得把簡報延期至明天。

突破盲點!!

Cancel 是「取消」的意思，依句意應改用 postpone「延期」。

Track 16

063 錯誤 If you want to listen to some music, I can **open** the stereo.

正確 If you want to listen to some music, I can **turn on** the stereo.

中譯 如果你想聽音樂，我可以把音響打開。

突破盲點!!

「打開」有開關的東西（尤其是電器類）英文要用 turn on，「關掉」則用 turn off，不可用 open 和 close。

064 錯誤 Are you **seeing** any interesting programs on TV?

正確 Are you **watching** any interesting programs on TV?

中譯 你在看有趣的電視節目嗎？

突破盲點!!

See 為「看見、看到」之意，一般不用進行式；「觀看」應用 watch 表達，可用進行式。

065 錯誤

Please **rise** the screen so I can see it.

正確

Please **raise** the screen so I can see it.

中譯 請把螢幕提高這樣我才看得到它。

突破盲點!!

Rise 為不及物動詞，意思是「上升」，raise 才是及物動詞，意思是「舉起、提高」。

066 錯誤

If we don't prepare for the negotiation, they will **win** us.

正確

1. If we don't prepare for the negotiation, they will **beat** us.

正確

2. If we don't prepare for the negotiation, they will **defeat** us.

中譯

1. 如果我們不準備好協商，他們會擊敗我們。
2. 如果我們沒有準備好協商，他們會打敗我們。

突破盲點!!

Win 可為不及物動詞，亦可作及物動詞，但作及物動詞用時，其受詞不可為「人」，只可為「事物」，如：win a war、win a game、win a prize 等。要表「勝過（對方）」應用 beat 或 defeat。

Track 17

067

A: Where's the boss?

錯誤	B: He has **out**. He'll be back soon.
正確	B: He has **gone out**. He'll be back soon.

中譯 A：老闆在哪裡？ B：他出去了，很快就會回來。

突破盲點!!

Out 是副詞，has out 無意義，「出去」應當說成 go out，而本句為「現在完成式」，故改成 has gone out。

068

錯誤	He **learned** most of his knowledge of the fashion industry by working with his uncle, a famous designer.
正確	He **gained** most of his knowledge of the fashion industry by working with his uncle, a famous designer.

中譯 藉由和他的名設計師叔叔一起工作，他獲取了他大部分的時尚產業知識。

突破盲點!!

「學習知識」是中文的講法，英文應說 gain knowledge「獲取知識」。

069 錯誤 I **hope I could** figure out a new marketing strategy.

正確 1. **I wish I could** figure out a new marketing strategy.

正確 2. **I hope I can** figure out a new marketing strategy.

中譯 1. 但願我可以想出一個新行銷策略。
2. 我希望我可以想出一個新行銷策略。

突破盲點!!

Wish 和 hope 不同，前者通常表示「不可能實現或難以實現的願望」，hope 則表示「一般的希望、期望」，因此 wish 後的子句中動詞用「假設」語氣，而 hope 之後則否。

070 錯誤 I **like** to make an appointment for next week.

正確 I **would like** to make an appointment for next week.

中譯 我想約下星期見面。

突破盲點!!

I like to 與 I would (I'd) like to 意義與用法不同；前者的意思是「我喜歡做……」，後者則用來表示說話者「想做……」，是客氣、委婉的一種表達方式。

Track 18

B. 動詞形式的錯誤 Verb Form Errors

a. IRREGULAR VERBS

071

The government **buyed** many computer screens from us last year.

The government **bought** many computer screens from us last year.

中譯　政府去年向我們買了很多電腦螢幕。

Buy 為不規則動詞，其三態為 buy、bought、bought。

072

錯誤

I am sorry. We've **selled out**.

正確

I am sorry. We've **sold out**.

中譯　對不起，我們已經賣完了。

突破盲點!!

Sell 是不規則動詞，其三態為：sell、sold、sold。另，sell out 是「賣完」的意思。

073 錯誤 The DVD **got stucked** when I tried to eject it.

正確 The DVD **got stuck** when I tried to eject it.

中譯 DVD 在我試著要退出片子時卡住了。

突破盲點!!

Stuck 為動詞 stick 的過去式和過去分詞，不須再加 ed。另，「卡住了」可用 be stuck 或 get stuck 表達。

b. AGREEMENT

074 錯誤 My company always **expect** me to work on weekends.

正確 My company always **expects** me to work on weekends.

中譯 我的公司總是希望我可以在週末工作。

突破盲點!!

Company「公司」是單數名詞，做主詞時動詞需採第三人稱單數形，即在原形動詞後加 s。

Track 19

075

錯誤 A lot of potential customers **is** not happy with our decision.

正確 A lot of potential customers **are** not happy with our decision.

中譯　很多潛在客戶都不滿意我們的決定。

突破盲點!!

Customer「客戶」為普通名詞，本句中它以複數出現在主詞位置，故動詞須採複數形的 are。

076

錯誤 **What's** the advantages of this material?

正確 **What are** the advantages of this material?

中譯　這種材質有些什麼優點？

突破盲點!!

本句為疑問句，而主詞並非句首的疑問詞 what，而是 the advantages，故動詞用 are。

077 錯誤 Everybody at the workshop **were** very happy.

正確 Everybody at the workshop **was** very happy.

中譯 研討會上的每個人都很開心。

突破盲點!!

Everybody、somebody、anybody 和 nobody 等複合字皆視為單數，故動詞用第三人稱單數的 was。

078 錯誤 The shipment of T-shirts **were** delayed for one week.

正確 The shipment of T-shirts **was** delayed for one week.

中譯 T 恤的運送遲到了一個星期。

突破盲點!!

本句的主詞為 the shipment，of T-shirts 為介系詞片語，作形容詞用，修飾前面之主詞；因主詞為單數，故動詞應用 was。

Track 20

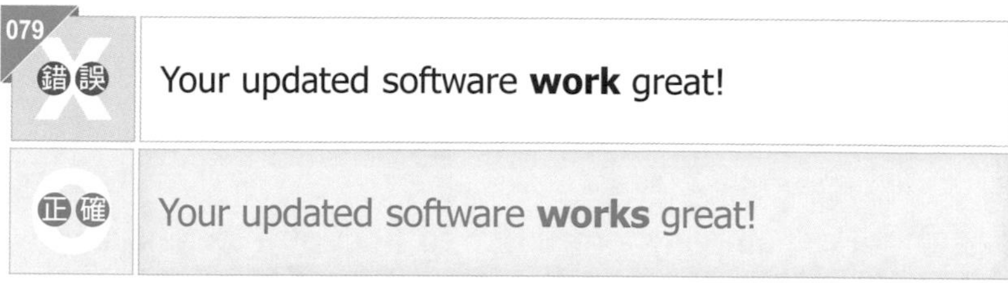

079

錯誤 Your updated software **work** great!

正確 Your updated software **works** great!

中譯　你的更新軟體非常好用！

Software 一般視為物質名詞，作主詞時動詞須用「第三人稱、單數」。

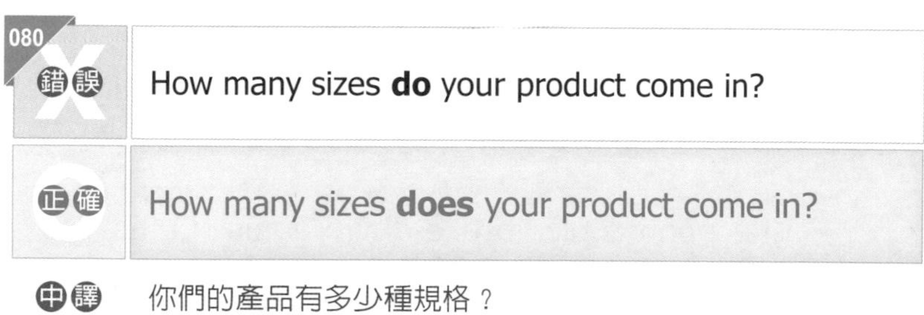

080

錯誤 How many sizes **do** your product come in?

正確 How many sizes **does** your product come in?

中譯　你們的產品有多少種規格？

注意本句的主詞並非 sizes，而是 (your) product，因此助動詞應用第三人稱單數的 does。

c. INFINITIVES

081

錯誤 The company forced him **accept** a lower salary.

正確 The company forced him **to accept** a lower salary.

中譯 這家公司強迫他接受較低的薪資。

突破盲點!!

本句中的 forced 為一普通動詞，其受詞 him 必須用不定詞 to + V 做為補語，否則句中就會有兩個動詞，不合文法。

082

錯誤 The photocopier broke down again. Could you manage **repairing** it?

正確 The photocopier broke down again. Could you manage **to repair** it?

中譯 影印機又壞了。你能設法修好它嗎？

突破盲點!!

在 manage 後遇到動詞時，要改為不定詞 (to V) 形式，不可用動名詞 (Ving)。

Track 21

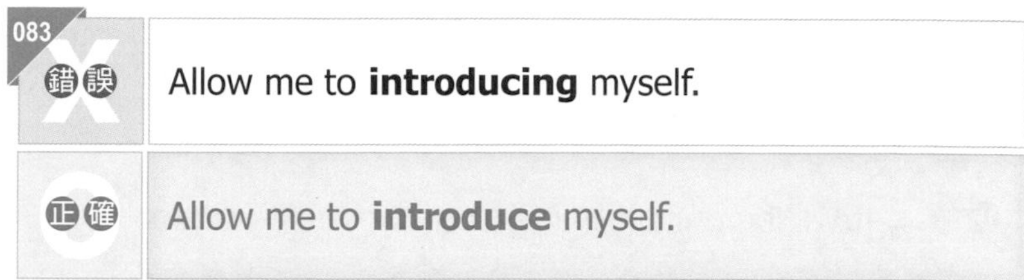

083

錯誤　Allow me to **introducing** myself.

正確　Allow me to **introduce** myself.

中譯　容我介紹我自己。

突破盲點!!

本句中之 to 為不定詞的 to，非介系詞 to，故其後用原形動詞。

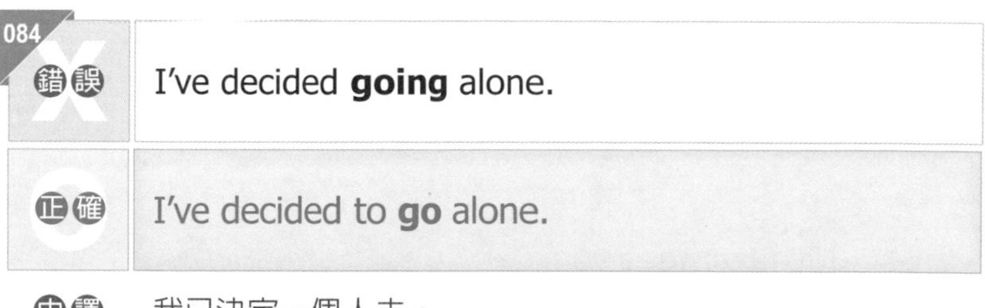

084

錯誤　I've decided **going** alone.

正確　I've decided to **go** alone.

中譯　我已決定一個人去。

突破盲點!!

在動詞 decide 之後需用不定詞 (to V)，不可用動名詞 (Ving)。

085

錯誤 It will be our pleasure **treating** you to dinner.

正確 It will be our pleasure **to treat** you to dinner.

中譯 能請你吃晚餐是我們的榮幸。

本句的 It 為假主詞，而不定詞與動名詞雖皆可用假主詞代替，但因主要動詞為未來式，故應選表「將」發生的不定詞，而非「已」發生的動名詞。

086

錯誤 Nice **meet** you.

正確 Nice **to meet** you.

中譯 很高興認識你。

Nice to meet you. 為 It's nice to meet you. 的省略式；換言之，不定詞片語 to meet you 原為真主詞，to 不可任意省略。

Track 22

d. ACTIVE / PASSIVE

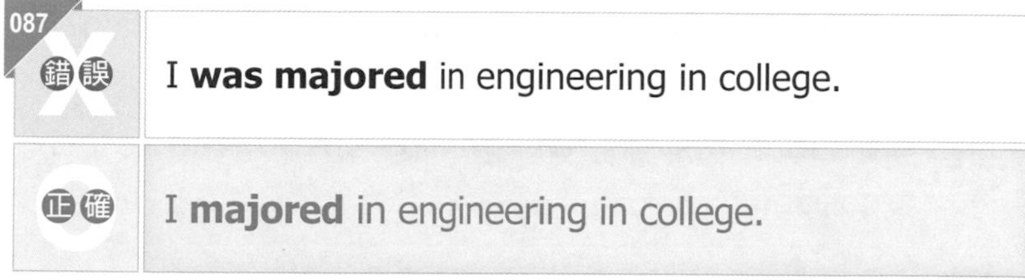

中譯　我大學主修工程學。

Major 當動詞，應用主動式。另，major 亦可當名詞用，如：I am an English major.。

中譯　我舉起手臂時會痛。

Hurt 表「感到疼痛」時，應用主動式，不用被動式。

089 錯誤

If Linda resigns, will you **promote** to her position?

正確

If Linda resigns, will you **be promoted** to her position?

中譯 如果琳達辭職，你會被升遷到她的職位嗎？

Promote 為一及物動詞，原則上應有其受詞，但因本句為被動式，「被」升遷者 you 轉為主詞。

090 錯誤

The soap **can use** to clean anything in your home.

正確

The soap **can be used to** clean anything in your home.

中譯 這塊肥皂可以用來清洗你家中的任何東西。

本句主詞 The soap 為「被」使用之物，故應用被動式動詞。

Track 23

091

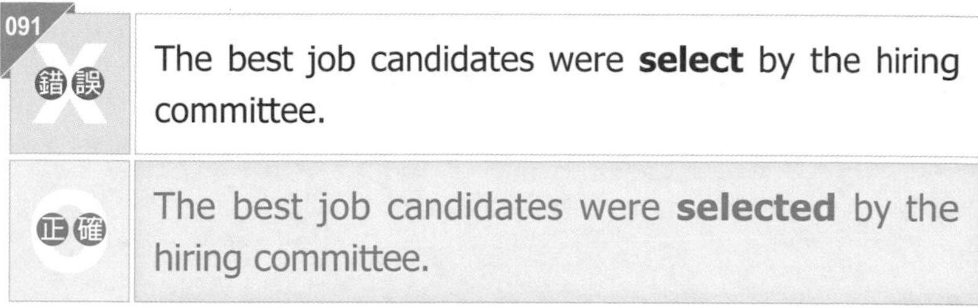

中譯　最佳職務人選由聘僱委員會選出。

突破盲點!!

Select 為動詞，不可直接置於 be 動詞 were 之後，應將其改為過去分詞，構成被動式。

092

錯誤　The report was **sending** to all the senior executives.

正確　The report was **sent** to all the senior executives.

中譯　這份報告被送給所有的資深主管。

突破盲點!!

本句主詞是 the report，為一「事物」，故動詞應採「被動」，而非主動（過去進行式）。

093 錯誤 Were you **borned** in England?

正確 Were you **born** in England?

中譯 你是在英國出生的嗎？

突破盲點!!

動詞 bear 有兩個過去分詞：born 和 borne； 前者用於被動式，後者則用於完成式。

e. PARTICIPLES

094 錯誤 I am **call** to talk to your accounts department.

正確 I am **calling** to talk to your accounts department.

中譯 我打電話來找你們的會計部門。

突破盲點!!

Am call 為錯誤動詞組合，如主動詞 call 之前用 be 動詞 am，應將 call 改為現在分詞，構成現在進行式。

Track 24

095

Their new stationery product line is coming out next month. I **look forward to see** it.

Their new stationery product line is coming out next month. I **look forward to seeing** it.

中譯 他們新款文具產品下個月就要問世了。我非常期待看到它。

動詞片語 look forward to 中的 to 是介系詞的 to，而非不定詞的 to，因此其後應接名詞，若遇動詞則改為動名詞，不可用原形動詞。

096

My first point **is relating** to the environment cleanup effort.

My first point **is related** to the environmental cleanup effort.

中譯 我第一個重點和整頓環境的努力有關。

「與……有關」應用 be related to 表達，be relating to 形成進行式「正在與……有關」，不合理。

097

錯誤 Do you hear the train **to come**?

正確 Do you hear the train **coming**?

中譯 你聽到火車來了嗎？

Hear 為一「感官動詞」，其後受詞之補語可為原形動詞或現在分詞；因本句指火車「正在」來，故選用 coming。

098

錯誤 Do you want to **go to bowling** with me?

正確 Do you want to **go bowling** with me?

中譯 你想和我去打保齡球嗎？

Go 後用現在分詞表「去從事某項活動」，如：go shopping、go swimming、go hunting 等。

Track 25

f. UNNECESSARY VERBS

中譯　K-Mart 再也不存在了。

突破盲點!!

Exist 為動詞，非形容詞，不可再使用其他動詞。另，注意主詞 K-Mart 為第三人稱單數，故動詞加 s。

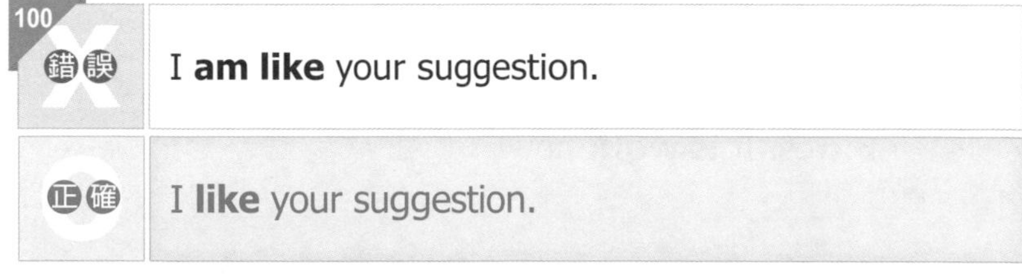

中譯　我喜歡你的建議。

突破盲點!!

Like 當「喜歡」時為動詞，不可再用其他動詞，作「像」解時為介系詞，應加動詞，如：Don't talk like that.。

101

錯誤 We **are agree** with your proposal.

正確 We **agree** with your proposal.

中譯 我們同意你的提案。

突破盲點!!

Agree 本身即為動詞，不須再使用 be 動詞。

102

A: Did you repair the computer yet?

錯誤 B: Yes. It **is work** now!

正確 B: Yes. It **works** now!

中譯 A：你修電腦了嗎？
B：是的。現在可以用了！

突破盲點!!

機器、器官等的「運作」，英文用動詞 work 表達；因主詞 it 為第三人稱單數，故加 s。

Track 26

Please consider purchasing our new software. It is so fast and therefore **is save** time.

Please consider purchasing our new software. It is so fast and therefore **saves** time.

中譯　請考慮購買我們的新軟體。它非常快速因此可省時。

And 為對等連接詞，用來連接 is 和 saves 兩個動詞（主詞為 it）；is save 為錯誤動詞結構。

I will contribute everything I **can do** to your recycling efforts.

I will contribute everything I **can** to your recycling efforts.

中譯　我會盡我所能協助你做回收工作。

原句中的助動詞 do 是多餘的，如使用會顯得累贅，故應予刪除。

g. MISSING/INCOMPLETE VERBS

105

錯誤 Let's **back** to the first paragraph.

正確 Let's **go back** to the first paragraph.

中譯 讓我們回到第一段。

突破盲點!!

以 Let's (Let us) 起頭的句子為祈使句，其後應接動詞，而 back 並非動詞，是副詞。

106

錯誤 This policy is too general and **no focus**.

正確 This policy is too general and **has no focus**.

中譯 這個政策太籠統沒有重點。

突破盲點!!

And 為對等連接詞，必須連接前後對等之文法結構；general 為形容詞而 focus 為名詞，不對等，因此將 no focus 改為與 is too general 對等之動詞片語結構 has no focus。

Track 27

107

錯誤 What time will you **sleep** tonight?

正確 What time will you **go to sleep** tonight?

中譯 你今晚幾點會睡？

突破盲點!!

Sleep 雖然可以譯為「睡覺」，但一定要「睡著」才算，本句問的應是幾點鐘「去」睡覺，故應加 go to。

108

A: I am so worried about my progress report.

錯誤 B: You always get a good score. Don't **concern** about it.

正確 B: You always get a good score. Don't **be concerned** about it.

中譯 A：我很擔心我的進度報告。
B：你總是得到很好的成績。不用擔心。

突破盲點!!

動詞 concern 是「與……有關」、「使（人）擔心」的意思；動詞片語 be concerned about 則指「（為某事）擔心」。

109 錯誤 I will consult with my boss when I **back** to Taiwan.

正確 I will consult with my boss when I **go back** to Taiwan.

中譯 我回台灣時會跟我的老闆商量。

由 when 引導的是一（副詞）子句，故需有動詞，而 back 是副詞，因此得加上動詞 go。

h. OTHER

110 錯誤 We can let you **to replace** your order.

正確 We can let you **replace** your order.

中譯 我們可以讓你更換你的訂貨。

本句中的 let 為一使役動詞，其受詞 you 的補語須用原型動詞，即，將不定詞的 to 省略。

Track 28

111 錯誤 She made us **to leave** the office because we were too noisy.

正確 She made us **leave** the office because we were too noisy.

中譯 她讓我們離開辦公室因為我們太吵了。

Make 在本句中為使役動詞，其受詞補語須使用原形動詞。

112 錯誤 When I was young, I **ever learned** piano.

正確 When I was young, I **learned** piano.

中譯 我年輕時學過鋼琴。

Ever 雖有「曾經」的意思，不過通常只用於疑問句、否定句或條件句 (if 子句)，如：Have you ever been to Japan?、I don't remember ever seeing him before.、If you are ever in Taipei, do come and see me.。

113

錯誤　I **have ever** been to Canada.

正確　I **have** been to Canada.

中譯　我去過加拿大。

突破盲點!!

Ever 只能用在疑問句、否定句和條件句中。

114

錯誤　Would you like to **marry with** a Taiwanese woman?

正確　Would you like to **marry** a Taiwanese woman?

中譯　你想娶個台灣女人嗎？

突破盲點!!

Marry 作「嫁」、「娶」時，其後直接跟嫁、娶的對象（受詞），不須用介系詞。

Track 29

115

錯誤 Please come to my house **for having** dinner sometime.

正確 1. Please come to my house **to have** dinner sometime.

正確 2. Please come to my house **for** dinner sometime.

中譯 1. 請找個時間到我家吃晚餐。
2. 請找個時間到我家享用晚餐。

突破盲點!!

在 come 之後，可用「to + V」或「for +名詞」表目的。

116

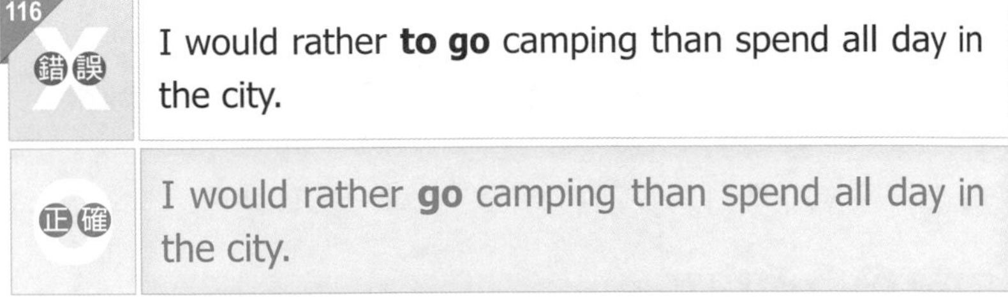

錯誤 I would rather **to go** camping than spend all day in the city.

正確 I would rather **go** camping than spend all day in the city.

中譯 我寧可去露營也不願整天待在都市裡。

突破盲點!!

在 would rather 之後需用原形動詞。另，注意 than 之後也用原形動詞。

117 錯誤 I **suggest you to** try green tea instead of black tea.

正確 I **suggest that** you try green tea instead of black tea.

中譯 我建議你不要喝紅茶，改喝綠茶。

突破盲點!!

動詞 suggest 不直接以「人」當受詞，其後可接名詞、動名詞或 that 子句。（注意，若 suggest 之後為 that 子句，此子句的動詞要用原形動詞。）

118 錯誤 He **recommended that we placed** a smaller order.

正確 He **recommended that we place** a smaller order.

中譯 他建議我們下小一點的訂單。

突破盲點!!

Recommend 的受詞為 that 子句時，該子句中的動詞必須使用原形動詞。（英式英語則在動詞前加 should。）

Track 30

119 錯誤

You can **setting** the temperature by pressing this button.

正確

You can **set** the temperature by pressing this button.

中譯 你可以按這個按鈕來設定溫度。

在情態助動詞（如：can、could、may、would 等）後，應用原形動詞；在作助動詞用的 be 動詞後才能出現現在分詞（構成現在進行式）。

120 錯誤

I **should to be** free to help you later today.

正確

I **should be free** to help you later today.

中譯 我今天晚點時應該有空幫你。

Should 屬情態助動詞，其後接原形動詞，不可接不定詞。

121

錯誤 It's a long way. We can take **turn** driving.

正確 It's a long way. We can take **turns** driving.

中譯 路途很遠，我們可以輪流開車。

突破盲點!!

Take turns 是「輪流」的意思，注意須用複數形 turns。

122

錯誤 **Welcome you** to our corporate headquarters!

正確 1. **We welcome you** to our corporate headquarters!

正確 2. **Welcome** to our corporate headquarters.

中譯 1. 我們非常歡迎你來我們的總公司。
2. 歡迎（你）來我們的總公司。

突破盲點!!

Welcome 可為動詞，亦可作形容詞；若其後為受詞則為動詞用法，若無則為形容詞用法。Welcome you ... 為命令句，不合理，應加主詞 We；或將 welcome 做形容詞，把 you 去掉。

Track 31

123

錯誤 If we **offer** a five percent discount, they **would** accept the offer.

正確 1. If we **offer** a five percent discount, they **will** accept the offer.

正確 2. If we **offered** a five percent discount, they **would** accept the offer.

中譯 1. 如果我們提供百分之五的折扣，他們將會接受報價。
2. 如果我們提供百分之五的折扣，他們就會接受報價。

突破盲點!!

若 if 子句之動詞為現在式，主要子句之動詞前用助動詞 will；若 if 子句為過去式，主要子句則用 would。前者表達「可能」的情況，後者表「假設」（與現在事實相反）的情況。

124

錯誤 He's good but seems to **lack of** confidence.

正確 He's good but seems to **lack** confidence.

中譯 他很不錯，但似乎缺乏自信。

突破盲點!!

Lack 做動詞用時，一般為及物，其後直接用受詞，不須加介系詞 of。（注意，lack 作名詞用時則須 of，如：a lack of confidence。）

125 錯誤 She **determines** to be the manager someday, and I think she will succeed.

正確 She **is determined** to be the manager someday, and I think she will succeed.

中譯 她決心有一天要當上經理，我也認為她會成功。

「下定決心要做某事」通常用 be determined to do 表達；原句使用現在簡單式動詞 determines 不妥，因現在簡單式一般用來表達「不變」的事實。

C. 動詞時態的錯誤 Verb Tense Errors

a. PRESENT TIME

126 錯誤 Our portable stereo **is including** batteries.

正確 Our portable stereo **includes** batteries.

中譯 我們的手提音響包含電池。

突破盲點!!

Include 並非動態動詞，不應使用進行式，應改為簡單式。

Track 32

127

A: Can your company furnish us with fog lights?

錯誤 B: We **didn't** produce fog lights.

正確 B: We **don't** produce fog lights.

中譯 A：你們公司可以提供我們霧燈嗎？
B：我們並不生產霧燈。

突破盲點!!

此對話之「情境」為「現在」，動詞一律使用現在式，故將 didn't 改為 don't。

128

錯誤 As you **could** see from the schedule, we only have one hour for the factory tour.

正確 As you **can** see from the schedule, we only have one hour for the factory tour.

中譯 一如你在計劃表看到的，我們只有一小時參觀工廠。

突破盲點!!

本句情境為「現在」，而 could 為 can 之過去式，不適用本句。注意，could(和 would 類似) 有時可表「客氣」，如用於請求時：Could you do me a favor?。

129

錯誤 Thanks for sharing your ideas with me. I **had learned** many things from you.

正確 Thanks for sharing your ideas with me. I **have learned** many things from you.

中譯 謝謝你和我分享你的想法。我已經從你那兒學到很多東西。

突破盲點!!

從本例中之第一句話可知，正確情境為「現在」，即「至目前為止已經」，故用現在完成式。

130

錯誤 Have you ever **get** a late invoice from them?

正確 Have you ever **got** a late invoice from them?

中譯 你有從他們那拿到遲來的發票嗎？

突破盲點!!

Get 為不規則動詞，其三態為 get、got、got/gotten，本句為現在完成式，主動詞應使用過去分詞。

Track 33

131

錯誤 I **am** a managing director for only one year.

正確 I **have been** a managing director for only one year.

中譯 我只當了一年管理主任。

突破盲點!!

本句中有表時間長短之片語 for only one year，意指「從去年到現在」，故應用現在完成式，而非現在簡單式。（注意，片語中之 for 可省略）。

132

錯誤 I **divide** my presentation into four main points.

正確 I **have divided** my presentation into four main points.

中譯 我已經把我的報告分成四大要點。

突破盲點!!

本句中雖無明顯時間副詞，但依句意「分」的動作目前已完成，故用現在完成式。

We have **improve** our product every year for the last five years.

We have **improved** our product every year for the last five years.

中譯　過去五年來我們每一年都改良我們的產品。

本句的時間副詞若只為 every year，則動詞用現在簡單式，但本句動作發生的時間是「過去五年來的每一年」，故應用現在完成式。

We **are** in the shoe business since 1995.

正確

We **have been** in the shoe business since 1995.

中譯　從一九九五年以來我們就從事鞋業了。

突破盲點!!

Since 1995 意思是「自一九九五年至今」，故動詞應用現在完成式。

Track 34

135 錯誤 My company **is always** well-known for its top quality tools.

正確 1. My company **is** well-known for its top quality tools.

正確 2. My company **has always been** well-known for its top quality tools.

中譯 1. 我公司以高品質的器具出名。
2. 我公司一直都是以高品質的器具而出名。

突破盲點!!

Always是一「頻率副詞」，一般用來修飾動詞（如：He always comes late.），如用來修飾形容詞，依然有表「頻率」的功能（如：He is always late.）本句的形容詞well-known不適合用always修飾，應予刪除，或將be動詞改成「現在完成」形式，表示「一直都是」亦可。

136

錯誤 Recently we **are** working on a new computer project.

正確 Recently we **have been** working on a new computer project.

中譯　最近我們一直在做一個新的電腦專案。

突破盲點!!

Recently 是「近來、最近」的意思，恰當的動詞時態應為現在完成進行式，而非現在進行式。

137

錯誤 I **am studying** English since high school.

正確 I **have been studying** English since high school.

中譯　我從高中就一直在念英文了。

突破盲點!!

句中有 since high school，指「從過去到現在」，因此用現在完成進行式。

Track 35

b. PAST TIME

138

I had **placed** the order last week, so they must have received it by now.

I **placed** the order last week, so they must have received it by now.

中譯　我上星期下了訂單，所以他們現在一定收到了。

本句中出現一明確過去時間 last week，故動詞應用過去簡單式，無須使用過去完成式。

139

A: Did you contact the American buyer yet?

錯誤　B: My secretary **had sent** a letter yesterday.

正確　B: My secretary **sent** a letter yesterday.

中譯　A：你和美國的買家聯絡了嗎？
B：我的秘書昨天寄信了。

突破盲點!!

本對話之情境為「過去」，又 B 之回答中用了 yesterday，故動詞用過去簡單式即可。

140 錯誤 We **have invested** a lot of money in the new project last month.

正確 We **invested** a lot of money in the new project last month.

中譯 我們上個月在新方案上投資了很多錢。

突破盲點!!

原句中有時間副詞 last month，表明為在「過去」所發生的事，故動詞應採過去式，而非現在完成式。

141 錯誤 He almost **go crazy** when we told him the bad news.

正確 He almost **went crazy** when we told him the bad news.

中譯 我們告訴他這個壞消息時，他幾乎抓狂了。

突破盲點!!

本句中有一表「過去時間」之 when 子句，故主要子句之動詞應用過去式。

Track 36

142

錯誤 Last weekend I **did** nothing but **watched** TV.

正確 Last weekend I **did** nothing but **watch** TV.

中譯 上個週末我什麼都沒做只看電視。

突破盲點!!

在 nothing but 後應用原形動詞，故將 watched 改為 watch。

143

A: I didn't see you yesterday.

錯誤 B: I stayed home because I **was having** a headache.

正確 B: I stayed home because I **had** a headache.

中譯 A：我昨天沒看到你。
B：我待在家裡因為我頭痛。

突破盲點!!

身體的疼痛不屬動作，一般不用「進行式」，而用「簡單式」表達。

144

錯誤 **Do** you have lunch yet?

正確 **Did** you have lunch yet?

中譯 你吃過午餐了嗎？

突破盲點!!

如「吃過午餐」，應該是「過去」的事，因此助動詞用過去式。

145

錯誤 When did they **told** you about the salary increase?

正確 When did they **tell** you about the salary increase?

中譯 他們什麼時候告訴你要加薪的？

突破盲點!!

本句為疑問句，過去式的概念已經由助動詞 did 表達，told 須還原。

Track 37

146 錯誤 If I **had** the money then, I would buy the house.

正確 If I **had had** the money then, I would have bought the house.

中譯 假如當時我有錢，就把房子買下了。

本句表達的是與過去事實相反的假設，if 子句須用過去完成式，主要句子在 would 之後則接現在完成式。

147 錯誤 I **was used to worry** a lot when I worked in the finance division.

正確 I **used to worry** a lot when I worked in the finance division.

中譯 我以前在財務部門工作時常常很焦慮。

Used to 後接原形動詞表「過去的習慣或狀態」。

148

Sorry for the interruption. Let me finish what I was **say**.

Sorry for the interruption. Let me finish what I was **saying**.

中譯　很抱歉被打斷了。請讓我把話說完。

Say 為動詞，不應置於過去式 be 動詞 was 之後，如將其改為現在分詞 saying，則構成過去進行式。

149

I apologize that we didn't **went** to the ceremony last night.

I apologize that we didn't **go** to the ceremony last night.

中譯　我為我們昨晚沒去典禮道歉。

本句中 that 子句表達的動作發生在過去 (last night)，但「過去」的概念已在表否定的過去式助動詞 didn't 中表達，故動詞用原形。

Track 38

150 錯誤 Last night I **must** stay up late and prepare the annual report.

正確 Last night I **had to** stay up late and prepare the annual report.

中譯 昨晚我必須熬夜準備年度報告。

突破盲點!!

助動詞 must 本身無過去式，可用其同義詞 have to 之過去式 had to 來表達。

151 錯誤 Did you know he **was died** last year?

正確 Did you know he **died** last year?

中譯 你知道他去年過世了嗎？

突破盲點!!

Die 為動詞，並無被動式；本句既指明死於去年，應用過去式。

c. FUTURE TIME

152

If we have to return the product, **what** happen?

If we have to return the product, **what will** happen?

中譯　如果我們得退回產品，會發生什麼事呢？

條件句（if 子句）須以現在式代替未來式，故主要子句之動詞應以未來式呈現。

153

After they **will sign** the contract, let's go out for drinks.

After they **sign** the contract, let's go out for drinks.

中譯　他們簽約後，我們就出去喝幾杯。

在表時間的副詞子句中，要用現在式來代替未來式。

Track 39

D. 片語動詞 Phrasal Verbs

a. PARTICLE ERRORS

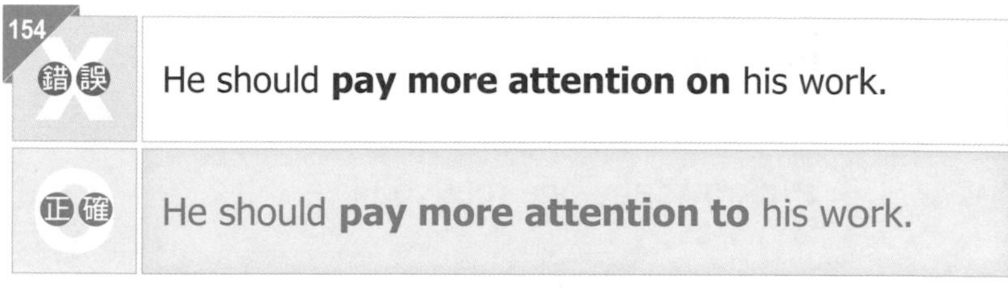
154

錯誤 He should **pay more attention on** his work.

正確 He should **pay more attention to** his work.

中譯 他應該更專注於他的工作。

Pay attention to 的 to 表專注的對象，為固定的介系詞，不可任意更改。

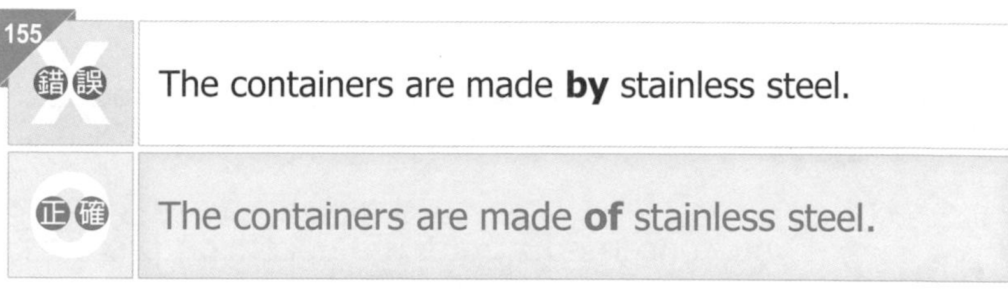
155

錯誤 The containers are made **by** stainless steel.

正確 The containers are made **of** stainless steel.

中譯 這些容器是不銹鋼製造的。

突破盲點!!

「用……製造的」是 be made of ...，而非 be made by ...。

156

A: These diamond rings are beautiful.

錯誤 B: **Pick up** any one that you like.

正確 B: **Pick out** any one that you like.

中譯 A：這些鑽石戒指很漂亮。
B：挑任何一個你喜歡的。

突破盲點!!

Pick up 是「撿起、拾起」的意思，本句中應用 pick out，指「挑選」。

157

錯誤 Are you concerned **with** the upcoming product trials?

正確 Are you concerned **about** the upcoming product trials?

中譯 你在擔心即將來臨的產品測試嗎？

突破盲點!!

Be concerned with 是「與……有關」的意思，而 be concerned about 則是「擔心……」，不可混淆。

Track 40

158

錯誤 Their service is inferior **than** ours.

正確 Their service is inferior **to** ours.

中譯 他們的服務比我們的差。

突破盲點!!

Inferior是「劣的、差的」的意思，不是「比較級」，故其後不跟than，而必須跟介系詞to。

159

錯誤 You can open the cover **by** a screwdriver.

正確 You can open the cover **with** a screwdriver.

中譯 你可以用螺絲起子打開蓋子。

突破盲點!!

介系詞by表「方法、手段」，with則指「使用（工具）」；原句亦可改為You can open the cover by using a screwdriver.。

b. TRANSITIVE VERBS

160

錯誤 Please **consider about** our offer.

正確 Please **consider** our offer.

中譯 請考慮我們的出價。

本句中 consider 為一及物動詞，其後直接跟受詞，不須使用介系詞 about。（注意，不可將 consider 與 think about 混淆。）

161

錯誤 We would like to **discuss about** your business proposal.

正確 We would like to **discuss** your business proposal.

中譯 我們想討論你的交易提案。

Discuss 為一及物動詞，其後直接跟受詞，不須使用介系詞 about。（注意，不可將 discuss 與 talk about 混淆。）

Track 41

162 錯誤 Did the boss **mention about** the invoices?

正確 Did the boss **mention** the invoices?

中譯 老闆有提到發票的事嗎？

Mention 為一及物動詞，其後直接跟受詞，不須加介系詞。

163 錯誤 I want to **stress on** the importance of on-time delivery.

正確 I want to **stress** the importance of on-time delivery.

中譯 我想要強調準時運送的重要性。

Stress 為一及物動詞，其後不須加介系詞 on，但若做名詞用則加 on（to put/place/lay stress on something）。

164

When you give your presentation, please **emphasize on** the need for motivation.

When you give your presentation, please **emphasize** the need for motivation.

中譯 當你做簡報時，請強調動機的必要性。

Emphasize 為及物動詞，其後不須介系詞 on，但其名詞 emphasis 之後則需加介系詞（to put/place/lay emphasis on something）。

165

We will **contact with** you as soon as we receive your order.

We will **contact** you as soon as we receive your order.

中譯 我們一接到您的訂單就會儘快與您聯絡。

Contact 為及物動詞，其後直接跟受詞，但若做名詞時則須用介系詞，如：We have lost contact with John.

Track 42

166

錯誤 Your colleague **accompanied with** me to the movie last night.

正確 Your colleague **accompanied** me to the movie last night.

中譯 你同事昨晚陪我去看電影。

突破盲點!!

Accompany 為一及物動詞，其後直接跟受詞，不須加介系詞。

167

錯誤 Alexander always **requests for** extra work when he is not busy.

正確 Alexander always **requests** extra work when he is not busy.

中譯 亞歷山大不忙時都會要求額外的工作。

突破盲點!!

Request 是一及物動詞，其後不須跟介系詞 for，但是若做名詞用其後則須用介系詞 (make a request for)。

168

錯誤 Could you **write down**?

正確 Could you **write it down**?

中譯 你可以把它寫下來嗎？

突破盲點!!

Write為一及物動詞，其後必須跟受詞，如本句之write it down。

169

錯誤 Do you **like**?

正確 Do you **like it**?

中譯 你喜歡它嗎？

突破盲點!!

Like是及物動詞，必須有受詞，其受詞可為名詞（如：I like English.）、代名詞（如本句）、動名詞（如：I like dancing.）或不定詞（如：I like to read.）。

Track 43

170 錯誤 This lotion smells great. I will **introduce** to my friends.

正確 This lotion smells great. I will **introduce it** to my friends.

中譯 這個乳液聞起來很香。我會把它介紹給我朋友。

突破盲點!!

Introduce 是及物動詞，其後須接受詞；本例中先提及 lotion，再提及時為避免重複，而用代名詞 it 代替之。

c. INTRANSITIVE VERBS

171 錯誤 We need everyone to **participate** the trade show.

正確 We need everyone to **participate in** the trade show.

中譯 我們需要每個人都參加貿易展。

突破盲點!!

Participate 為不及物動詞，其後通常跟介系詞 in，表「參加、參與」之意。

172

錯誤 Please don't **laugh** me.

正確 Please don't **laugh at** me.

中譯 請不要嘲笑我。

突破盲點!!

Laugh「笑」為不及物動詞，不可直接加受詞；laugh at 有「嘲笑」的意思。（若 laugh 要作及物用，其受詞必須為同源受詞，如：He laughed a bitter laugh.「他苦笑」。）

173

錯誤 We are eagerly **waiting** your response to our offer.

正確 We are eagerly **waiting for** your response to our offer.

中譯 我們殷切等待你對我們出價的回應。

突破盲點!!

動詞 wait 一般當不及物用，其後應接介系詞；wait for 即「等待」之意。

Track 44

174 錯誤 She has been **waiting** me for thirty minutes.

正確 She has been **waiting for** me for thirty minutes.

中譯 她已經等了我三十分鐘。

突破盲點!!

Wait「等待」為不及物動詞，其後常跟介系詞 for。(若等待的對象為「機會、輪次」時，可作及物用，如 wait one's turn。)

175 錯誤 Do you like **listening** music?

正確 Do you like **listening to** music?

中譯 你喜歡聽音樂嗎？

突破盲點!!

Listen「聽」為不及物動詞，不可直接加受詞，必須先加介系詞 to。注意，不要將 listen 與 see「聽見、聽到」混淆；後者是及物動詞。

d. VERBS USED WITH PREPOSITIONS

176

錯誤 Did you **prepare** the negotiation yet?

正確 Did you **prepare for** the negotiation yet?

中譯 你有沒有為協商作好準備？

突破盲點!!

Prepare 作及物動詞解時，意思是「準備」；作不及物動詞解（其後接介系詞 for）時，則指「為……作準備」。本句指「為協商作準備」，故需加介系詞 for。

177

錯誤 Let me **comment** your suggestion.

正確 Let me **comment on** your suggestion.

中譯 讓我對你的提議做評論。

突破盲點!!

Comment 為不及物動詞，其後不可直接跟受詞，應先加介系詞 on。

Track 45

178

錯誤 I **insist** the cooperation of everyone on the team.

正確 I **insist on** the cooperation of everyone on the team.

中譯 我堅持團隊中每個人都必須互助合作。

突破盲點!!

Insist 作不及物動詞時，其後接介系詞 on，再接受詞（名詞或動名詞）；作及物動詞時，其後需接「that 子句」。

179

錯誤 The staff always **complains** the long working hours.

正確 The staff always **complains about** the long working hours.

中譯 職員常抱怨工作時間太長。

突破盲點!!

Complain 作不及物動詞時，要先加介系詞 about 再接受詞；作及物動詞時，其受詞應為「that 子句」。

180

錯誤 Tom always **objects** Helen's ideas.

正確 Tom always **objects to** Helen's ideas.

中譯 湯姆總是反對海倫的意見。

「對……表示異議」在 object 後須用介系詞 to 再接受詞，意即此時 object 為不及物動詞；若 object 作及物用，其受詞則必須是「that 子句」。

181

錯誤 Will you **apply** a new job?

正確 Will you **apply for** a new job?

中譯 你會申請新工作嗎？

突破盲點!!

Apply 指「申請」時為不及物動詞，其後常跟介系詞 for；但若 apply 作「應用」解時，則為及物動詞，其後直接接受詞。

Track 46

182

錯誤 Don't **worry** it.

正確 Don't **worry about** it.

中譯 不用擔心。

突破盲點!!

Worry 作「擔心」解時，為不及物動詞，後接介系詞 about；作「令人擔心」解時，則為及物，受詞為「人」，如：He often worries his parents.「他常令父母操心」。

183

A: Why haven't the speakers been fixed yet?

錯誤 B: I **explained** to you already.

正確 B: I **explained it** to you already.

中譯 A：為什麼麥克風還沒有修好呢？
B：我已經跟你解釋過了。

突破盲點!!

Explain 可為及物或不及物，但在此簡短對話中，因 A 明白提出一問題，而 B 表示已針對「該問題」作過解釋，故在 explain 後用受詞 it 來指該問題，語意較清楚、完整。

184 錯誤 I have to **search** the solution.

正確 I have to **search for** the solution.

中譯 我必須尋求解決方案。

突破盲點!!

Search 作及物動詞時，指「搜查」，而 search for 則指「尋找、探求」。

185 錯誤 Do you **agree** me?

正確 Do you **agree with** me?

中譯 你贊同我嗎？

突破盲點!!

動詞 agree 之後可接介系詞、不定詞或 that 子句，但不可直接跟受詞。

Track 47

e. IDIOMATIC PHRASAL VERBS

186 錯誤 We need to **pay careful attention** what the team leader says.

正確 We need to **pay careful attention to** what the team leader says.

中譯 我們要特別注意組長說的話。

突破盲點!!

Pay attention to 是固定用法，介系詞 to 不可少，而其後則為其受詞。

187 錯誤 The chemical company wants to **enter** an agreement with us.

正確 The chemical company wants to **enter into** an agreement with us.

中譯 這家化學工廠想和我們簽署協議。

突破盲點!!

動詞 enter 是「進入」的意思，而片語 enter into 則指「著手處理（某事）」。

188

錯誤 Don't **focus** this problem so much.

正確 Don't **focus on** this problem so much.

中譯 不用太專注於這個問題。

突破盲點!!

Focus（與 concentrate 相同）後應用介系詞 on。

189

錯誤 Yesterday I went to the store to **try** some new clothes.

正確 Yesterday I went to the store to **try on** some new clothes.

中譯 昨天我去店裡試穿一些新衣服。

突破盲點!!

「試穿」英文用 try on，為一固定片語用法。

Track 48

190

錯誤 I have to **find out** some information about our Internet connection.

正確 I have to **find** some information about our Internet connection.

中譯 我得找些我們網路連線的資料。

片語 find out 是「發現」之意，而動詞 find 則指「找」；依句意應採用後者。

NOTES

3

名詞
Nouns

A. 錯選名詞 Noun Choice Errors

B. 名詞形式的錯誤 Noun Form Errors

C. 數量與複數 Number/Plurals

D. 可數與不可數 Countable/Uncountable

E. 限定詞 Determiners

F. 代名詞 Pronouns

G. 動名詞 Gerunds

H. 子句 Clauses

A. 錯選名詞 Noun Choice Errors

191

錯誤 Our educational videos will increase your sales **effect**.

正確 Our educational videos will increase your sales **effectiveness**.

中譯 我們的教學錄影帶會有效提高你們的銷售力。

突破盲點!!

Effect 指的是因做某事而產生的「結果、效果」，例如：The TV commercial didn't have much effect on sales.「那支電視廣告對銷售量並沒有起多大作用。」Effectiveness 則指某個方法之「有效、有力」，如本句中之 increase your sales effectiveness。

192

錯誤 How much is the bus **fee**?

正確 How much is the bus **fare**?

中譯 搭公車的費用是多少錢？

突破盲點!!

Fee 指「服務費」、「手續費」、「學費」、「入會費」等；「車費」、「船費」、「飛機票價」等則用 fare。

Track 49

193 錯誤 I couldn't sleep last night, so I have no **power** this morning.

正確 I couldn't sleep last night, so I have no **energy** this morning.

中譯 我昨晚睡不著，所以我今天早上沒氣力。

突破盲點!!

Power 指事物的「力量」或人的「權力」;講人的「氣力、精力」應該用 energy。

194 錯誤 We have to pay a **fee** to use this highway.

正確 We have to pay a **toll** to use this highway.

中譯 我們使用這條高速公路必須付費。

突破盲點!!

使用道路、港口等必須付的「通行費」叫 toll，不是 fee。

195

錯誤 The restaurant is too crowded today. There are too many **clients**.

正確 The restaurant is too crowded today. There are too many **customers**.

中譯　今天餐廳太擠了。有好多客人。

Client 指「委託人」、「客戶」；一般商店的客人應用 customer。

196

錯誤 I live near a church, so sometimes I see a **father** walking by.

正確 I live near a church, so sometimes I see a **priest** walking by.

中譯　我住教堂附近，所以有時會看到神父走過。

突破盲點!!

Father 作「神父」解時，一般都是直接稱呼，且 f 須用大寫，如：Father (Smith)；priest 則指一般的神父（天主教）或牧師（基督教）。

Track 50

197

A: Do you like flying?

錯誤 B: Not really. The **chairs** are too small for me.

正確 B: Not really. The **seats** are too small for me.

中譯 A：你喜歡搭飛機嗎？ B：不很喜歡。座位對我來說太小了。

突破盲點!!

「固定的座位」是 seat；chair 是「（可移動的）椅子」。

198

錯誤 I **learned** some interesting **subjects** in the seminar.

正確 1. I **learned** some interesting **things** in the seminar.

正確 2. I **studied** some interesting **subjects** in graduate school.

中譯 1. 我在研討會學了些有趣的事。
2. 我在研究所研習了一些有趣的科目。

突破盲點!!

Learn「學習」的受詞應該是 things「事物」，而 study「研習」的對象則為 subject「科目」。

199

錯誤 If the machine breaks down within a year, we will fix it free of **cost**.

正確 If the machine breaks down within a year, we will fix it free of **charge**.

中譯 如果機器在一年內壞掉，我們會免費修理。

Cost 指「購物時的花費」，而 charge 則指「被索取的費用」。

B. 名詞形式的錯誤 Noun Form Errors

200

A: You can come to my house for dinner.

錯誤 B: Are you a good **cooker**?

正確 B: Are you a good **cook**?

中譯 A：你可以來我家吃晚餐。
B：你是個好廚師嗎？

Cooker 指「烹飪用具」（如鍋、爐等），cook 才是「廚師」，不可混淆。

Track 51

201

錯誤 I see **you mean**.

正確 1. I see **your meaning**.

正確 2. I see **what you mean**.

中譯 我懂你的意思。

突破盲點!!

See 在本句中作及物動詞用，其後應接受詞，而 you mean 為主詞+動詞的句子結構，不可當受詞，可改為名詞結構 (your meaning) 或名詞子句 (what you mean)。

202

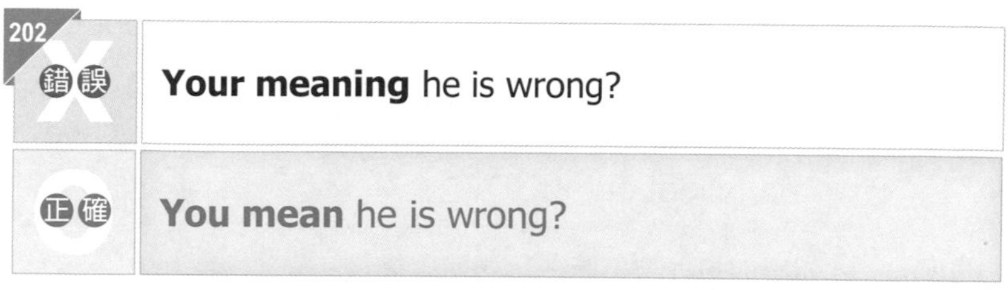

錯誤 **Your meaning** he is wrong?

正確 **You mean** he is wrong?

中譯 你的意思是他是錯的囉？

突破盲點!!

中文的「你的意思是……」英文應用 you mean ...，即用主詞+動詞的結構表達，不可直譯為 your meaning。

203 錯誤 It is so hot. I am sorry that my apartment has no **air condition**.

正確 I am sorry that my apartment has no **air-conditioning/conditioner**.

中譯 很抱歉我的公寓沒有冷氣。

Air-conditioning 指「空調(系統)」；冷氣機則叫做 air-conditioner。

204 錯誤 If you want **something** special price, we can talk about it.

正確 1. If you want **a** special price, we can talk about it.

正確 2. If you want **something at a** special price, we can talk about it.

中譯 1. 如果你想要特惠價，我們可以談談。
2. 如果你想要某物的特惠價，我們可以談談。

突破盲點!!

Special price 的結構是形容詞＋名詞，構成一名詞片語，不可反過來修飾 something（但 something special 成立），可改成 a special price 或 something at a special price。

Track 52

C. 數量與複數 Number/Plurals

205

The **point** we have to consider today are liability and insurance.

The **points** we have to consider today are liability and insurance.

中譯 我們今天要考慮的重點是責任和保險。

Be動詞屬連綴動詞，其後為主詞補語；本句中之補語為 liability and insurance，是「兩」項事物，故主詞應為複數。

206

The **followings** are the main points to be discussed.

The **following** are the main points to be discussed.

中譯 以下是討論的重點。

The following的意思可為單數或複數，但其本身採單數形，不可加s。

207 錯誤 We are pleased about the recent sales **figure**.

正確 We are pleased about the recent sales **figures**.

中譯 我們對於最近的銷售數據非常滿意。

突破盲點!!

Figure 雖是一可數名詞（即可以為單數或複數），但講「數據」時一般常用複數。

208 錯誤 I am a **salespeople**.

正確 I am a **salesperson**.

中譯 我是一名銷售員。

突破盲點!!

People 指「人們」，本身為複數；因本句主詞是 I，故改成 person。另，注意 salesperson 中的 sale 之後有 s。此外，I am a sales. 則是另一個常見的錯誤說法。

Track 53

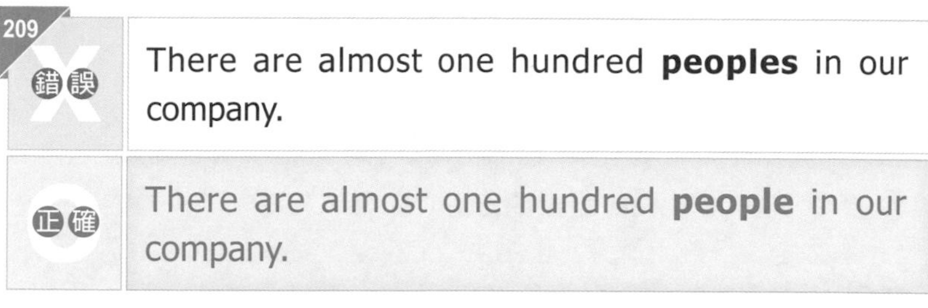
209

錯誤 There are almost one hundred **peoples** in our company.

正確 There are almost one hundred **people** in our company.

中譯　我們公司有將近一百人。

突破盲點!!

People 是「人們」的意思，本身就為複數，不用再加 s；但，注意 people 若作「民族」解時，則可用單、複數，如：a peace-loving people、the peoples of Asia。

210

A: Do you like stinky tofu?

錯誤 B: Of course! I am **Taiwanese people**.

正確 B: Of course! I am a **Taiwanese person**.

中譯　A：你喜歡臭豆腐嗎？ B：當然！我是台灣人。

突破盲點!!

People 指的是「人們」，一定是兩個人以上，句中只指一個人，若一定要說「人」，則必須使用 person。此外，更普遍的說法是使用形容詞的形式：I'm Taiwanese.。

211 錯誤 I have three **childs**.

正確 I have three **children**.

中譯 我有三個小孩。

突破盲點!!

Child 為一不規則名詞，其複數形為 children，並非直接加 s。

212 錯誤 **Every customers like** to watch the chef cook.

正確 1. **Every customer likes** to watch the chef cook.

正確 2. **All the customers like** to watch the chef cook.

中譯 1. 每個顧客都喜歡看主廚下廚。
2. 所有的顧客都喜歡看主廚下廚。

突破盲點!!

Every 是「每一個」的意思，其後只能用單數名詞；若要表「所有的」則應選用 all。

D. 可數與不可數 Countable/Uncountable

213

錯誤 This company requires too **many** hard **works**.

正確 This company requires too **much** hard **work**.

中譯 這家公司的工作過度繁重。

Work 為不可數名詞，故不可加 s，因此也不可用 many 修飾。（注意，homework 和 housework 亦不可數。）

214

錯誤 Can you give us any **advices** about how to market the product?

正確 Can you give us any **advice** about how to market the product?

中譯 你們可以給我們任何有關要如何銷售這個產品的意見嗎？

突破盲點!!

Advice 為一不可數名詞，故不可使用複數形；但若要數它，可在前使用量詞 piece，如：a piece of advice。

215

You've given me a lot of good **advices** recently.

You've given me a lot of good **advice** recently.

中譯　你最近給了我很多好意見。

Advice 為不可數名詞，無複數，若要表「幾個」意見或忠告，可使用量詞 piece，如：two pieces of advice。

216

Our intern is supposed to conduct **a market research**.

Our intern is supposed to conduct **market research**.

中譯　我們的實習生應該進行市場調查。

Research 一般作不可數名詞，故不可加不定冠詞 a。

Track 55

217

In my professional **views**, the photos in the catalog will not attract anyone's attention.

In my professional **view**, the photos in the catalog will not attract anyone's attention.

中譯 以我專業的眼光來看，目錄裡的照片不會吸引任何人的目光。

In one's view 和 in one's opinion 兩片語中的 view 和 opinion 都不用複數。

218

We have **many evidences** of unethical activities undertaken by our competitor.

正確

We have **a lot of evidence** of unethical activities undertaken by our competitors.

中譯 我們有很多我們競爭者卑鄙活動的證據。

Evidence 為不可數名詞，不可加 s，亦不可用 many 修飾。（注意，常用的 information 亦為不可數名詞。）

219

We need to buy a lot of **furnitures** for the new office.

We need to buy a lot of **furniture** for the new office.

中譯 我們的新辦公室需要購買很多家具。

Furniture 為不可數名詞，沒有複數形，不能加 s。（注意，另一類似字 equipment「設備、器材」亦不可數。）

220

The director has told us **a good news** about his negotiation.

The director has told us **good news/some good news** about his negotiation.

中譯 主任已經告訴我們關於他協商的好消息。

News 為一不可數名詞，其前不可用不定冠詞 a，但可用 some，因 some 可修飾可數名詞，也可修飾不可數名詞。

Track 56

221

錯誤 I heard **a** good news yesterday.

正確 I heard **some** good news yesterday.

中譯 我昨天聽到一些好消息。

突破盲點!!

News 為不可數名詞，若要指「一則消息」或「一條新聞」，則可用 a piece of news 來表達。

222

錯誤 Our factory is stocked with brand new **equipments**.

正確 Our factory is stocked with brand new **equipment**.

中譯 我們的工廠有全新的設備。

突破盲點!!

Equipment 為不可數名詞，無複數形，不可加 s。

223 錯誤 We need to read **these** consumer **mails** as soon as possible.

正確 We need to read **this** consumer **mail** as soon as possible.

中譯　我們必須儘快看這封消費者的來信。

突破盲點!!

Mail 指「郵件」，為不可數名詞，不可加 s。注意，不可將 mail 與 letter 混淆，letter 是可數名詞。

224 錯誤 One of our **staffs** is always late.

正確 One of our **staff** is always late.

中譯　我們其中一個職員總是遲到。

突破盲點!!

Staff 是一個集合詞，指的是「全體職員」，不應該加 s。

Track 57

225

錯誤 I like your **characters**.

正確 I like your **character**.

中譯 我喜歡你的個性。

突破盲點!!

Character 指一個人的「性格」時不可數，但若指「角色」時則是可數名詞，如：the characters in the novel。

226

錯誤 The earthquake caused a lot of **damages**.

正確 The earthquake caused a lot of **damage**.

中譯 地震造成多處損害。

突破盲點!!

Damage 指「損害」時不可數，但注意作「損害賠償金」解時，則一定要用複數形 damages。

227

錯誤

It is **a hard work** to prepare all of these emergency orders.

正確

It is **hard work** to prepare all of these emergency orders.

中譯　要備妥這些所有的緊急訂單是項艱難任務。

突破盲點!!

Work 是不可數名詞，因此其前不可加不定冠詞 a；但 job 則為可數名詞，二者不可混淆。

228

錯誤

I need to paste this poster on the wall.
Could you get me **a glue**?

正確

1. Could you get me **a bottle of glue**?

正確

2. Could you get me **some glue**?

中譯　我得將這幅海報貼在牆上。
1. 你可以幫我拿一瓶膠水來嗎？
2. 你可以幫我拿一些膠水來嗎？

突破盲點!!

Glue 為一物質名詞，不可數，故其前不可用不定冠詞 a；可改為 a bottle of glue 或 some glue。

Track 58

229

錯誤 I want to tell you **an important information** the manager just told me.

正確 I want to tell you **an important piece of information** the manager just told me.

中譯　我想告訴你一個經理剛告訴我的重要訊息。

Information 為一不可數名詞，其前不可使用不定冠詞 a，若要使用 a 則需要加量詞 piece。

230

錯誤 Let's have **a lunch** together today.

正確 Let's have **lunch** together today.

中譯　我們今天一起吃午餐吧。

Lunch 指一般午餐時為不可數名詞用，但在某些「特殊」情況下則可作普通名詞，如：a light lunch、a wonderful lunch、an early lunch 等。

E. 限定詞 Determiners

231

錯誤 It's too noisy outside. Would you close **door**?

正確 It's too noisy outside. Would you close **the door**?

中譯 外面好吵。你可以關上門嗎？

突破盲點!!

Door 為普通名詞，可數，故若非複數（在其後加 s），則其前必須有限定詞 (determiner)，如：a、the、this、that 等。

232

錯誤 I want to inquire about **laser printer** I purchased last week.

正確 I want to inquire about **the laser printer** I purchased last week.

中譯 我想要詢問關於我上星期購買的雷射印表機。

突破盲點!!

(Laser) printer 為可數名詞，又為單數，故須在其前使用限定詞 (determiner)，因本句明確表示為「上星期購買之印表機」，故在其前加定冠詞 the。

Track 59

233 錯誤	We would like you to attend **meeting** tomorrow.
正確	1. We would like you to attend **the meeting** tomorrow.
正確	2. We would like you to attend **a meeting** tomorrow.
正確	3. We would like you to attend **our meeting** tomorrow.

中譯
1. 我們希望你可以參加明天的那場會議。
2. 我們希望你可以參加明天的會議。
3. 我們希望你可以參加我們明天的會議。

Meeting 為可數名詞，其前須用限定詞，如定冠詞 the、不定冠詞 a 或所有代名詞 our 皆可。

234

錯誤 What **is difference between** these two versions?

正確 What **is the difference between** these two versions?

中譯 這兩個版本有什麼不同？

突破盲點!!

本句中明白指出是「這兩個版本之間」的不同，故 difference 前應用定冠詞。

235

錯誤 **Most of** factory workers think they are treated well.

正確 1. **Most of the** factory workers think they are treated well.

正確 2. **Most of our** factory workers think they are treated well.

中譯 1. 大部分的工廠員工認為他們受到好的待遇。
2. 我們大部分的工廠員工認為他們受到好的待遇。

突破盲點!!

當 most 作為「代名詞」時，其後常跟介系詞 of，但在 of 之後的名詞之「指稱」一定要「特定」，即在名詞前需要「特定指稱」的「限定詞」，如 the、my、these、those 等。（注意，同樣的情況也會出現在 many、some、any 等字之後。）

Track 60

236 錯誤 Have you read **all of** instructions for the new projector?

正確 Have you read **all of the** instructions for the new projector?

中譯 你有沒有讀新專案的全部程序指引？

若 all 後跟介系詞 of，則其後的名詞之指稱必須為「特定」，如加「定冠詞」、「所有格」、「指示詞」等。

F. 代名詞 Pronouns

(Introducing Benny)

237 錯誤 **He** is our sales agent, Benny.

正確 **This** is our sales agent, Benny.

中譯 （介紹班尼）這是我們的銷售代表班尼。

突破盲點!!

在介紹某人給某人認識時，不可用人稱代名詞 he，而應使用指示代名詞 this。

238 錯誤 Please sit down and **relax yourself**.

正確 Please sit down and **relax**.

中譯 請坐下來輕鬆一下。

突破盲點!!

Relax 作「放鬆身心」時為不及物動詞，其後不接受詞，包括「反身代名詞」。

239 錯誤 I can go to your office this afternoon, if **you are** convenient.

正確 I can go to your office this afternoon, if **it is** convenient.

中譯 如果（你）方便的話，我今天下午可以去你的辦公室。

突破盲點!!

「如果你方便」是中文的說法，英文 convenient 不可用來修飾「人」，只可指「狀況」。

Track 61

240

A: Wow, the streets are so crowded.

錯誤 B: Of course, **here** is Taiwan.

正確 B: Of course, **this** is Taiwan.

中譯 A：哇，街上都是人。 B：當然，這裡是台灣。

Here 是副詞，不可做主詞，應改為代名詞 this，表示「此處」、「本地」。

241

A: Does he know you?

錯誤 B: Yeah. I'm a **friend of him**.

正確 B: Yeah. I'm a **friend of his**.

中譯 A：他認識你嗎？ B：是的，我是他的一個朋友。

突破盲點!!

A friend of his 為所謂「雙重所有」，在介系詞 of（第一重所有）後應用所有代名詞（第二重所有）。如不用「雙重所有」可直接說 I'm his friend。

G. 動名詞 Gerunds

242

錯誤 Can we delay **to ship** the crates for two more days?

正確 Can we delay **shipping** the crates for two more days?

中譯 我們可以延後兩天運那些板條箱嗎？

突破盲點!!

一般在動詞 delay 後應接名詞或動名詞作為其受詞。類似的動詞包括 enjoy、mind、celebrate……等。

243

錯誤 The case is opened by **push** this button.

正確 The case is opened by **pushing** this button.

中譯 這個箱子是按這個按鈕打開的。

突破盲點!!

By 為介系詞，其後應有受詞，而動詞不能當受詞，須改成動名詞。

Track 62

Please check the power connection before **turn on** the machine.

Please check the power connection before **turning on** the machine.

中譯　請在啓動機器之前先檢查電源連接處。

Before 為介系詞，其後須接名詞作為受詞，如遇動詞則須改為動名詞。

Should we risk **to promote** the old product line?

正確

Should we risk **promoting** the old product line?

中譯　我們是否該冒險促銷舊款產品？

在某些及物動詞，如 risk、enjoy、mind 等之後若遇另一動詞，須將動詞改為動名詞的形式當受詞。

246

錯誤 We look forward to **hear** from your company.

正確 We look forward to **hearing** from your company.

中譯 我們非常期待貴公司的回應。

突破盲點!!

注意片語 look forward to 中的 to 為介系詞，其後應接受詞（名詞），本句中因其後原為一動詞，故須改為動名詞，才可做 to 的受詞。

247

錯誤 Would you mind **to explain** the operating procedure again?

正確 Would you mind **explaining** the operating procedure again?

中譯 你介意再解釋一次營運流程嗎？

突破盲點!!

Mind 作及物動詞用時，接名詞或動名詞作其受詞，不可用不定詞。

Track 63

248

錯誤 We can't avoid **to miss** the deadline.

正確 We can't avoid **missing** the deadline.

中譯 我們勢必趕不上截止時間。

突破盲點!!

某些動詞（如：avoid、enjoy、mind 等）其後如遇動詞，應改成動名詞型式，如本句中的 missing。

249

錯誤 I enjoy **to talk** with you about your innovative ideas.

正確 I enjoy **talking** with you about your innovative ideas.

中譯 我很喜歡和你討論你的創新點子。

突破盲點!!

Enjoy 為及物動詞，其後須接受詞，如遇動詞則須用動名詞，而非不定詞形式。

Do you remember **to cancel** the order yesterday?

正確 1. Do you remember **canceling** the order yesterday?

正確 2. Did you remember **to cancel** the order yesterday?

中譯 1. 你記得昨天取消訂單了嗎？
2. 你昨天記得要取消訂單嗎？

Remember 後若為 to V，其意思是「記得要去做（某事）」；其後若為 Ving，則指「記得做了（某事）」。

Thank you for **come** to our office on such short notice.

Thank you for **coming** to our office on such short notice.

中譯 謝謝你在接到通知後這麼短的時間內就到我們辦公室。

For 為介系詞，其後應接受詞，若碰到動詞，則須改成動名詞。

Track 64

252

錯誤 I enjoy **to walk** in the park.

正確 I enjoy **walking** in the park.

中譯 我喜歡在公園裡散步。

突破盲點!!

Enjoy 為一及物動名詞，其受詞必須是名詞或動名詞。

253

錯誤 Please stop **to say** that.

正確 Please stop **saying** that.

中譯 請不要那樣說。

突破盲點!!

Stop 後用不定詞表「停下來去做……」，用動名詞表「停止做……」。

The art museum is fantastic. It is worth **to see**.

正確 The art museum is fantastic. It is worth **seeing**.

中譯 美術館很棒，值得一看。

突破盲點!!

Worth 用於 be 動詞之後時，可視為一介系詞，其後必須跟名詞或動名詞。

I am used to **eat** alone now.

正確 I am used to **eating** alone now.

中譯 我現在習慣一個人吃。

突破盲點!!

Be used to 後接動名詞（或名詞）表「習慣於……」，注意此處的 to 為介系詞。

Track 65

256 錯誤

In addition to **give** a general introduction, the program also offers practical training.

正確

In addition to **giving** a general introduction, the program also offers practical training.

中譯 一般概論之外，該課程也提供實務訓練。

突破盲點!!

In addition to 中的 to 為介系詞，非不定詞的 to，故其後應接受詞，遇到動詞則改為動名詞。

257 錯誤

Due to **Maggie forgot** the contract, we could not conclude the negotiation.

正確

Due to **Maggie's forgetting** the contract, we could not conclude the negotiation.

中譯 由於梅琪忘了帶合約，我們沒有辦法結束協商。

突破盲點!!

Due to 為一片語介系詞，其後應接受詞，而 Maggie forgot the contract 為一完整句子，不可當受詞，應改成動名詞的結構。

258

錯誤 **After finish** this project, I want to move to another division.

正確 1. **After I finish** this project, I want to move to another division.

正確 2. **After finishing** this project, I want to move to another division.

中譯 1. 在我完成這個企劃案後，我要調到別的部門。
2. 完成這個企劃案後，我要調到別的部門。

突破盲點!!

After 可作連接詞或介系詞用，故其後不是子句，就應是受詞。

259

錯誤 Thanks for **your calling**.

正確 Thanks for **calling/your call**.

中譯 謝謝你的來電。

突破盲點!!

For 為介系詞，其後可接名詞或動名詞；若為動名詞則不須在其前使用所有格。

Track 66

260 錯誤 **Run** a meeting is not easy.

正確 **Running/To run** a meeting is not easy.

中譯 主持一個會議不容易。

突破盲點!!

Run 為動詞，不可當主詞，應改為動名詞 running 或不定詞 to run 形式。

H. 子句 Clauses

261 錯誤 No matter **they propose**, we will ask for a ten percent discount.

正確 No matter **what they propose**, we will ask for a ten percent discount.

中譯 不論他們的提案是什麼，我們都會要求百分之十的折扣。

突破盲點!!

No matter what/which/who/where/when/why/how「無論什麼／哪一個／誰／何處／何時／為什麼／如何」在句中具連接詞的功能，為固定用法，no matter 後之疑問詞不可任意省略。

262

The reason I am here is **because** I want to discuss the stock market.

The reason I am here is **that** I want to discuss the stock market.

中譯　我來這裡的原因是因為我想討論股市。

Because 為一從屬連接詞，用來引導表原因的副詞子句；本句中主要子句的主詞為 The reason，動詞為 is，其後應接主詞補語，而主詞補語應為名詞，不可為副詞，故將連接詞改為 that，即以名詞子句作主詞補語。（注意，本句主要子句主詞 The reason 後有一形容詞子句 I am here，而引導此子句的關係副詞 why 可省略。）

263

The problems **need to be resolved** are the defect ratio and the packaging delays.

The problems **that need to be resolved** are the defect ratio and the packaging delays.

中譯　有待解決的是瑕疵品比率和包裝延遲的問題。

本句主詞 The problems 之後為一關係子句（形容詞子句），因關係代名詞在該子句中具主詞之功能，故不可省略。

4

形容詞

Adjectives

264 錯誤 Your offer sounds good. We are very **interesting**.

正確 Your offer sounds good. We are very **interested**.

中譯 你的提議聽起來不錯。我們非常有興趣。

突破盲點!!

Interesting 是「有趣的」的意思，而 interested 才是指「感興趣的」。

265 錯誤 I feel so **boring** today.

正確 I feel so **bored** today.

中譯 我今天覺得很無聊。

突破盲點!!

Boring 指「令人覺得無聊的」，如：The book was very boring.；bored 則為「覺得無聊」。

Track 67

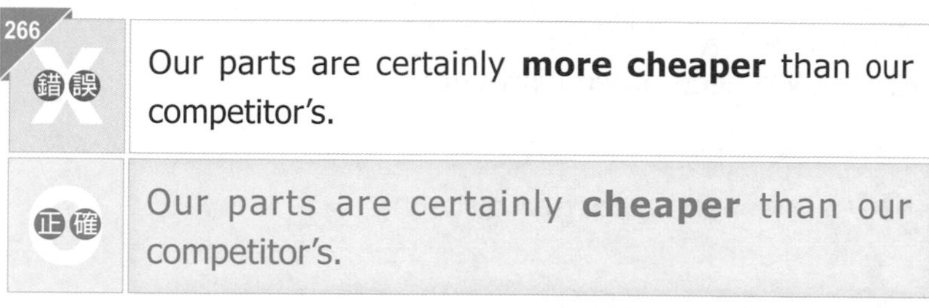

中譯　我們的零件當然比我們的競爭對手還要便宜。

突破盲點!!

Cheap 的比較級為 cheaper，不應在其前再加 more。注意，另一常見的錯誤是 more easier，同理 easy 的比較級為 easier，不須再用 more。

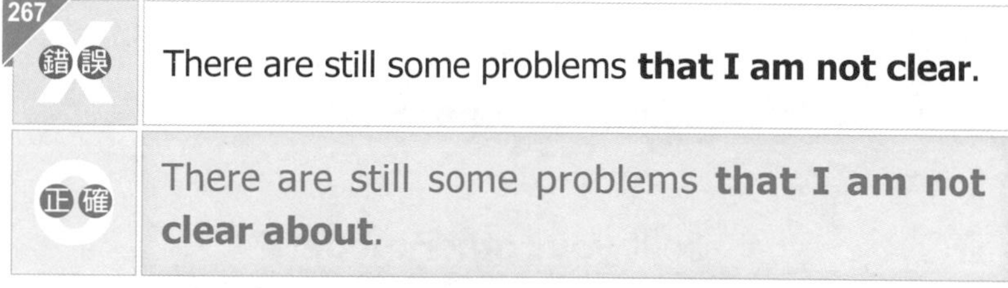

中譯　還是有些問題我不明瞭。

突破盲點!!

Clear 單獨使用時，意思是「清楚的」；clear about 則指「對……清楚」。

268

錯誤 We need **more** discount.

正確 We need **a larger** discount.

中譯 我們需要更多折扣。

突破盲點!!

中文「更多折扣」不可直譯為 more discount，應譯為 a larger discount。

269

錯誤 What about **your another model**?

正確 1. What about **your other model**?

正確 2. What about **your other models**?

中譯 1. 你們另一個款式如何？
2. 你們其餘的款式如何？

突破盲點!!

人稱代名詞所有格不可與 another（或 the other）連用，但可與 other 連用，而其後可為單數或複數名詞。

Track 68

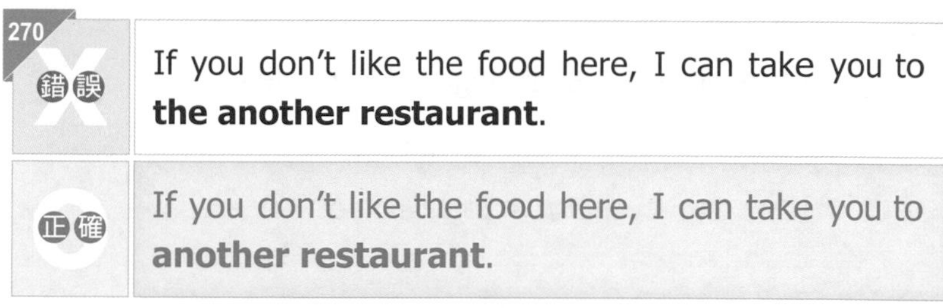

270

錯誤 If you don't like the food here, I can take you to **the another restaurant**.

正確 If you don't like the food here, I can take you to **another restaurant**.

中譯　如果你不喜歡這裡的食物，我可以帶你去另一家餐廳。

突破盲點!!

Another 為不定冠詞 an 和 other 的組合，表「不特定」的另一家，其前不可再加定冠詞 the。

271

錯誤 The boss seems less **happier** than he used to be.

正確 The boss seems less **happy** than he used to be.

中譯　老闆似乎比以前不快樂。

突破盲點!!

Less 為 more 的反義字，本身即表「比較」，因此其後之形容詞不須再用「比較級」。

272 錯誤 It's a **twelve hours** flight to Los Angeles.

正確 It's a **twelve-hour** flight to Los Angeles.

中譯 到洛杉磯的飛航要十二個小時。

突破盲點!!

Twelve- hour 的功能為形容詞，而英文的形容詞沒有複數；另注意 twelve 和 hour 之間要用連字號。

273 錯誤 I had a **childhood of carefree**.

正確 I had a **carefree childhood**.

中譯 我的童年無憂無慮。

突破盲點!!

Carefree 為形容詞，應用來修飾名詞 childhood。

Track 69

274

錯誤 You should feel **ashame** of yourself.

正確 You should feel **ashamed** of yourself.

中譯 你應該為你自己感到羞恥。

突破盲點!!

現代英文並無 ashame 這個字，只有 ashamed，為一形容詞。

275

A: Why did you come here?

錯誤 B: There is **no any** reason.

正確
1. B: There is **no** reason.
2. B: There is **not any** reason.
3. B: No reason.

中譯 A：你為何來這裡？
B：1. 沒有原因。 2. 沒有任何原因。 3. 沒原因。

突破盲點!!

No 和 any 不可連用，二者只能取其一，但 any 前可以用 not。

276 錯誤 I a little **afraid** to swim in the ocean.

正確 I **am** a little **afraid** to swim in the ocean.

中譯 我有點害怕在海邊游泳。

Afraid 是形容詞，在句中須跟動詞一起用，如：be afraid、look afraid 等。

277 錯誤 I **don't** busy recently.

正確 I **am not** busy recently.

中譯 我最近不忙。

Busy 為形容詞，不是動詞，故不可說 don't busy，其前應加動詞（如 be 動詞），再加否定動詞。

Track 70

278

錯誤 **Today** was too **tired**.

正確 1. **Today** was too **tiring**.

正確 2. Today **I** was **too tired**.

中譯 1. 今天真令人疲憊。
2. 我今天很累。

突破盲點!!

Tired 指「疲倦的」，用來形容「人」； tiring 指「令人疲憊的」，用來形容「事物」。

279

錯誤 There are so many **shoes** stores in Taiwan.

正確 There are so many **shoe** stores in Taiwan.

中譯 台灣有很多鞋店。

突破盲點!!

名詞+名詞構成複合名詞，由於前一名詞具形容詞的功能，因此不可用複數形，若整個複合名詞為複數，只能在後面的名詞用複數。

280

A: I am looking for my friend.

B: What does he look like?

錯誤	A: Well, he is wearing a **big and black** coat.
正確	A: Well, he is wearing a **big black** coat.

中譯　A：我在找我的朋友。

B：他什麼樣子？

A：他穿一件大的黑色外套。

突破盲點!!

Big 指「大小」，black 指「顏色」，屬不同類之形容詞，不應用對等連接詞 and 連接。（一般而言，屬性相同的形容詞才可用 and 連接，如：I am cold and hungry.。）

Track 71

281 錯誤 His rude remark was too **disgusted** for me to do anything about it.

正確 His rude remark was too **disgusting** for me to do anything about it.

中譯 他粗野的評論另我厭惡以致於我無法做出任何回應。

Disgusted 是由過去分詞（表被動）轉用的形容詞，是「感到厭惡」的意思，disgusting 則為由現在分詞（表主動）而來的形容詞，指「令人厭惡的」。

282 錯誤 Taipei is in **north Taiwan**.

正確 Taipei is **in northern Taiwan**.

中譯 台北位於北台灣。

North 通常指「北方的」，如：the north wind，而 northern 則指「（一地區之）北部的」。

283

錯誤 The tea is too **thick** for me.

正確 The tea is too **strong** for me.

中譯 這茶對我而言太濃了。

突破盲點!!

講飲料（如茶、咖啡）的「濃」，英文用 strong 表達；反之，表示「淡」則用 weak。

284

錯誤 The DVD players **are not enough**.

正確 1. **There are not enough** DVD players.

正確 2. We do not have enough DVD players.

中譯 1. 數位影音播放機不夠。
2. 我們沒有足夠的數位影音播放機。

突破盲點!!

本句所要表達的是現在「有」的 DVD 數量不夠，而不是 DVD 本身不夠，故不應以 DVD 為主詞，應使用存在句型（There + be）或明確表達是「誰」沒有足夠的 DVD。

Track 72

285 錯誤 I had a good time in Spain. It is a **funny** place.

正確 I had a good time in Spain. It is a **fun** place.

中譯 我在西班牙玩得很愉快。那是個好玩的地方。

突破盲點!!

Funny 是「好笑」的意思，表示「好玩」應用 fun。

286 錯誤 My colleague spent **all the** flight telling me about his children.

正確 My colleague spent **the whole** flight telling me about his children.

中譯 我同事花了整個飛行時間跟我談他的小孩。

突破盲點!!

「整個飛行時間」應用 the whole flight 表達；all the flight 不符英文使用習慣。

287 錯誤 You are **mistake** if you think the raw materials are low quality.

正確 You are **mistaken** if you think the raw materials are low quality.

中譯 如果你認為原料品質差的話，那你就錯了。

突破盲點!!

「弄錯了」英文要用 be mistaken 表示；mistaken 原是過去分詞，轉用成形容詞，意思是「弄錯的」

288 A: I still feel sick today.

錯誤 B: **You are so poor**.

正確 B: **Poor you**.

中譯 A：我今天還是覺得不舒服。

B：你真可憐。

突破盲點!!

You are so poor. 是「你很窮。」的意思；「你真可憐」要說 Poor you.。

Track 73

289

A: I can't find my favorite cologne, Jovan Musk at any of the department stores.

錯誤	B: Sogo has Jovan Musk **on sale**.
正確	B: Sogo has Jovan Musk **for sale**.

中譯 A：我在每家百貨公司都找不到我最喜歡的 Jovan Musk 古龍水。

B：Sogo 就有賣 Jovan Musk。

突破盲點!!

On sale 指「減價出售」，一般的販售應用 for sale。

290

A: How are things?

錯誤	B: Things are **well**.
正確	B: Things are **good**.

中譯 A：事情進行的如何？ B：還不錯。

突破盲點!!

Well 一般做副詞用，只有在表「身體健康」時才作形容詞用，故本句應改用形容詞 good。

NOTES

5

副詞
Adverbs

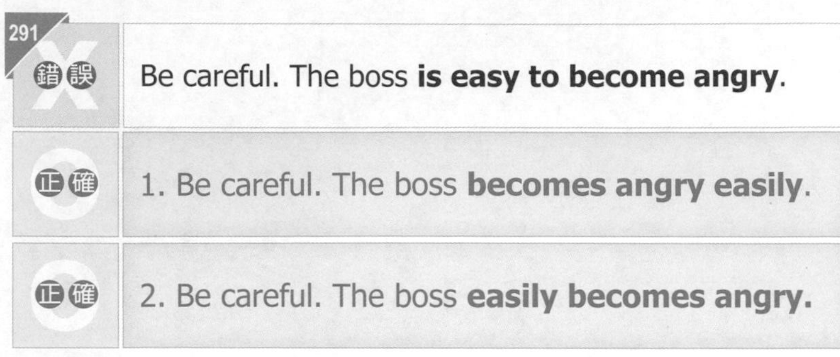

中譯　小心。老闆很容易就生氣。

突破盲點!!

英文的 easy「容易」不可直接用來修飾「人」，須注意。本句可將 easy 改成副詞 easily，用來修飾 become。

中譯　我很喜歡你的點子。

突破盲點!!

程度副詞 very 不可用來修飾動詞（一般只修飾形容詞或副詞），須改為 very much，置於句尾（正式文體中可置於動詞前）。

Track 74

293 錯誤 I **very like** your thinking.

正確 I **like** your thinking **very much**.

中譯 我非常喜歡你的想法。

突破盲點!!

Very 不可直接修飾動詞（注意，這與中文的「非常」用法不同），而必須用 very much，且必須置於句尾。

294 錯誤 I went to Hong Kong **for three times** last year to visit our regional office.

正確 I went to Hong Kong **three times** last year to visit our regional office.

中譯 我去年去香港三次視察我們在那個區域的公司。

突破盲點!!

There times 本身即可做副詞用（修飾 went），不須加介系詞 for。

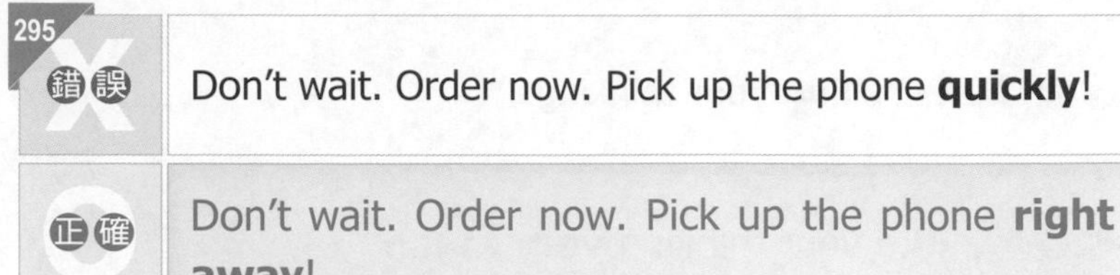

295

錯誤 Don't wait. Order now. Pick up the phone **quickly**!

正確 Don't wait. Order now. Pick up the phone **right away**!

中譯 別等了，現在就訂。馬上拿起電話！

突破盲點!!

Quickly 意思是「很快地、迅速地」，不符句意，應改用 right away「立刻、馬上」。

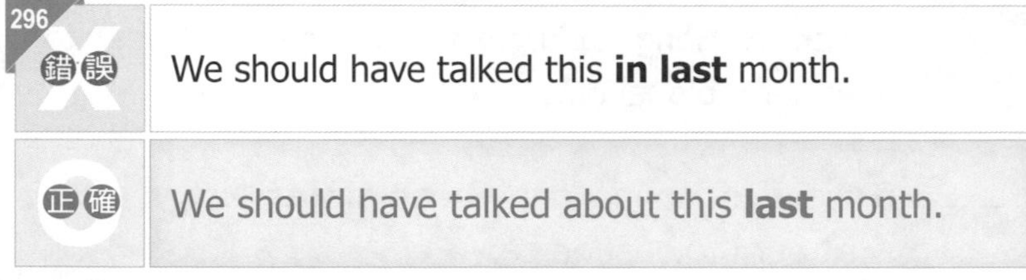

296

錯誤 We should have talked this **in last** month.

正確 We should have talked about this **last** month.

中譯 我們上個月應該已經討論過這個。

突破盲點!!

Last month、last year、last week、last night 等皆為（時間）副詞，其前不可加介系詞。

Track 75

297

錯誤 You have asked us some **recently** questions regarding our product catalog.

正確 **Recently**, you have asked us some questions regarding our product catalog.

中譯 最近你問了我們一些有關我們產品目錄的問題。

Recently 是一時間副詞，不可用來修飾名詞。注意，recently 通常與現在完成式連用。

298

A: I am from the East Coast.
B: Do you like living there?

錯誤 A: I **love there**!

正確 A: I **love it there**!

中譯 A：我是從東海岸來的。
B：你喜歡住在那裡嗎？
A：我非常喜歡！

突破盲點!!

There（和 here 同）為副詞，不可以當受詞，故加虛受詞 it。

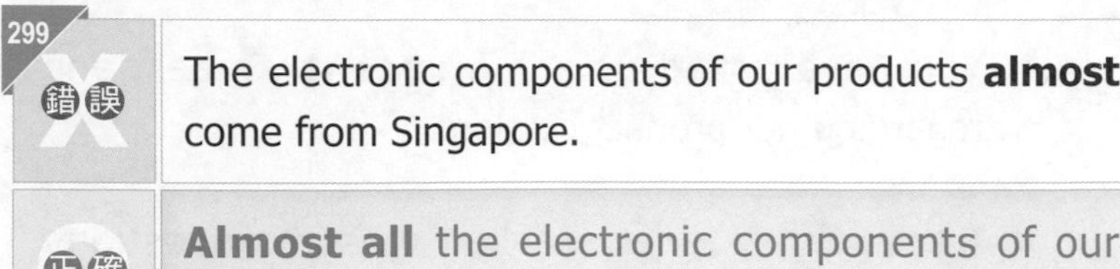

299

錯誤 The electronic components of our products **almost** come from Singapore.

正確 **Almost all** the electronic components of our products come from Singapore.

中譯 我們產品的電子零件幾乎全都來自新加坡。

突破盲點!!

Almost 的修飾對象為 all，並非動詞 come，故應置於 all 之前。（注意，不可因中譯而改變 almost 的位置。）

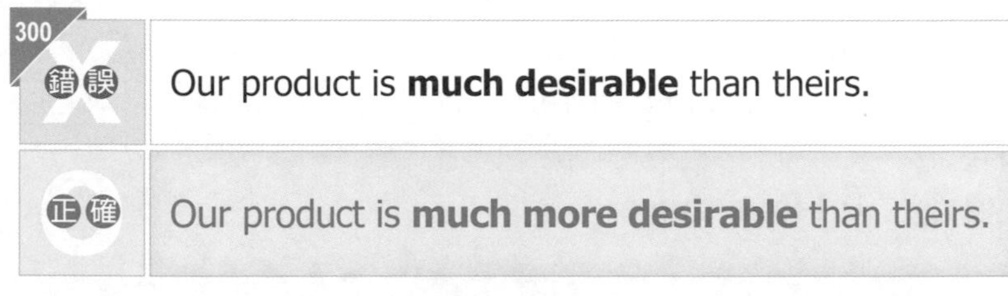

300

錯誤 Our product is **much desirable** than theirs.

正確 Our product is **much more desirable** than theirs.

中譯 我們的產品比他們的更理想。

突破盲點!!

原句中有 than，故可判斷全句應為一比較結構，因此在形容詞 desirable 前應有表示比較的副詞 more。

Track 76

301

錯誤 The boss told me that **for five times**!

正確 The boss told me that **five times**!

中譯 那件事老闆跟我說了五遍！

表示次數的字詞如 once、twice、five times 等為副詞，前面不需再用介系詞 for。

302

A: I just came back from a vacation in Australia.

錯誤 B: Did you have a nice time **at there**?

正確 B: Did you have a nice time **there**?

中譯 A：我剛從澳洲渡假回來。
B：你在那邊玩得愉快嗎？

突破盲點!!

There 為副詞，非名詞，其前不可用介系詞。

NOTES

6

介系詞
Prepositions

A. 表時間的介系詞 Prepositions of Time

B. 表位置的介系詞 Prepositions of Place

C. 其他介系詞 Other Prepositions

A. 表時間的介系詞 Prepositions of Time

303 錯誤

The weekly meetings should be held **at** the mornings.

正確

The weekly meetings should be held **in** the mornings.

中譯 每星期的例會應該在早上舉行。

In the morning(s) 為固定用法，介系詞必須用 in，但可以說 at down「破曉時」。

304 錯誤

He will work **at** the evening.

正確

He will work **in** the evening.

中譯 他將在晚上工作。

In the evening、in the morning 和 in the afternoon 為固定用法。另，at night、at dawn、at noon 和 at midnight 亦不可任意更改。

Track 77

305

錯誤 The new rule is that we cannot work in the office **in the night**.

正確 The new rule is that we cannot work in the office **at night**.

中譯 新規章是我們晚上不能在公司工作。

突破盲點!!

At night 和 in the evening 為固定用法，不可混淆。

306

錯誤 You can call us **during** 8 a.m. to 5 p.m.

正確 You can call us **from** 8 a.m. to 5 p.m.

中譯 你可以在早上八點到下午五點之間打電話給我們。

突破盲點!!

表達「從……到……」應用 from ... to ... 表達；during 指「在……期間」，如 during the day。

307

錯誤 Will you be open for business **at** New Year's Day?

正確 Will you be open for business **on** New Year's Day?

中譯 你們新年那天會營業嗎？

突破盲點!!

在「日」前的介系詞應用 on；at 指「時刻」，如：at 8:30、at 12:00。

308

錯誤 Let's talk about this problem **on** May.

正確 Let's talk about this problem **in** May.

中譯 我們五月再討論這個問題。

突破盲點!!

於「年」、「月」之前的介系詞應用 in，on 則用在「日」之前，如：on August 24、on Sunday 等。

Track 78

309 錯誤

Albert has been working on that project **since** three weeks.

正確

Albert has been working on that project **for** three weeks.

中譯　亞伯特三個星期以來一直在做那件專案。

如動詞是完成式，在句中的 since 後接「過去時間」(如：since yesterday)，而 for 則接「一段時間」(如本句中的 for three weeks)。

310 錯誤

Our company **started to produce** IC chips **since** 1995.

正確

1. Our company **has been producing** IC chips **since** 1995.

正確

2. Our company **started producing** IC chips **in** 1995.

中譯
1. 我們公司自一九九五年以來一直在製造晶片。
2. 我們公司在一九九五年開始製造晶片。

突破盲點!!

原句中有 since 1995「自一九九五年至今」，故不應使用過去式，而應用現在完成進行式；若要使用過去式，則應將時間改為 in 1995。

311 錯誤 I want to go to a hot spring **during** two days.

正確 I want to go to a hot spring **for** two days.

中譯 我想去泡兩天溫泉。

突破盲點!!

「For + 一段時間」表「為期或持續多久」；在說「某事在某一段時間之內發生」時，才用 during，如：I went swimming everyday during the summer.。

B. 表位置的介系詞 Prepositions of Place

312 錯誤 Ellen will call the office as soon as her plane **arrives Los Angeles**.

正確 Ellen will call the office as soon as her plane **arrives in Los Angeles**.

中譯 只要艾倫的飛機一抵達洛杉磯，她就會打電話到辦公室。

突破盲點!!

Arrive 為一不及物動詞，其後不可直接接受詞，需先加介系詞 in 或 at，再加受詞。

Track 79

313

A: Can you tell me where the Personnel Office is?

錯誤 B: It is **in** the second floor.

正確 B: It is **on** the second floor.

中譯 A：你可以告訴我人事部的辦公室在哪嗎？
B：在二樓。

突破盲點!!

表示「在第……樓」介系詞應用 on；in 一般用來指「在……裡」，如：in the office、in the building 等。

314

錯誤 We have a factory **on** Mainland China.

正確 We have a factory **in** Mainland China.

中譯 我們在中國大陸有間工廠。

突破盲點!!

在國家或大地區前介系詞一般用 in。

315

Can you give me some advice about the kinds of words to put **on** this rejection letter?

Can you give me some advice about the kinds of words to put **in** this rejection letter?

中譯　你可以建議我這封回絕信要放入哪些措詞嗎？

「在信中」或「在信上」英文用 in the letter 表達，不可說成 on the letter。

316

Please key in your data **at** the web site.

正確

Please key in your data **on** the web site.

中譯　請在網頁上鍵入你的資料。

猶如 write your name on the paper，本句應用 ... on the web site。

Track 80

This report is difficult to write. I've to put so many details **on** it.

This report is difficult to write. I have to put so many details **in** it.

中譯 這份報告很難寫。我必須加上很多細節。

與 in the book、in the newspaper、in the letter 同，in the report 才正確，不可說 on the report。

What time should we arrive **to** the airport?

正確 What time should we arrive **at** the airport?

中譯 我們幾點會到達機場？

「抵達」要用 arrive at 而不是 arrive to。若為較大的地方，則可使用 arrive in，如：arrive in New York。

319

錯誤 I didn't feel well yesterday, so I stayed **in** home.

正確 I didn't feel well yesterday, so I stayed **at** home.

中譯 我昨天覺得不舒服，所以待在家裡。

突破盲點!!

「待在家裡」要說 stay at home，而非 stay in home。但可以說 stay in the house。

320

錯誤 Cars drive **in** the right side of the road in Taiwan.

正確 Cars drive **on** the right side of the road in Taiwan.

中譯 在台灣汽車靠道路的右側行駛。

突破盲點!!

「在哪一邊」的介系詞用 on，不是 in。但如果講方向，則用 in，不用 on，如 in the east。

Track 81

321 錯誤 I didn't feel well yesterday, so I stayed **on** bed.

正確 I didn't feel well yesterday, so I stayed **in** bed.

中譯 我昨天覺得不舒服，所以待在床上。

突破盲點!!

In bed 是「睡覺、休息」的意思，不須用冠詞，為固定語法。

322 錯誤 What are you studying **in** the university?

正確 What are you studying **at** the university?

中譯 你在大學唸什麼？

突破盲點!!

In the university 較強調「地方」，而 at the university 則著重「活動」；換言之，前者指「在學校 (的範圍) 裡面」，後者則指「在學校求學」。

323

錯誤 My house is **nearby** the office.

正確 My house is **near** the office.

中譯 我家在公司附近。

突破盲點!!

Nearby 為形容詞，是「附近的」之意，如：a nearby city；near 則可作介系詞用，表示「在……附近」。

C. 其他介系詞 Other Prepositions

324

錯誤 Your question is too difficult **to** me.

正確 Your question is too difficult **for** me.

中譯 你的問題對我來說很困難。

突破盲點!!

本句介系詞應選用 for；原句使用的 to 通常用來表個人之「意見或感覺」，for 則表達個人之「能力」。試比較下列兩個句子。

1. The book is boring to me. 我覺得這本書很無聊。
2. The book is too boring for me to finish. 這本書太無聊我看不下去。

Track 82

325

錯誤 Can you tell me the reason **of** your complaint?

正確 Can you tell me the reason **for** your complaint?

中譯 你可以告訴我你抱怨的原因嗎？

突破盲點!!

「……的原由、理由」應用 the reason for 表達，而非 the reason of。

326

錯誤 My company is divided **by** two main divisions: research and product testing.

正確 My company is divided **into** two main divisions: research and product testing.

中譯 我的公司被分為兩大部門：研究部門和產品測試部門。

突破盲點!!

Be divided by 是「被……分割」之意，不適用於本句；應改為 be divided into「分成（若干部分）」。

327 錯誤 I heard the news **through** the radio.

正確 I heard the news **on** the radio.

中譯 我在收音機上聽到了那個消息。

突破盲點!!

與「在電視上」相同，「在收音機上」用介系詞 on，但注意 on the radio（與 listen to the radio 同）需要定冠詞 the。

328 錯誤 **According to** my opinion, the lease agreement is too strict.

正確 **In** my opinion, the lease agreement is too strict.

中譯 依我看來，這份租約太嚴格了。

突破盲點!!

According to「根據」的對象通常是別人（說的話）或其他資訊的來源，不可指自己或自己的意見。（According to me 亦為常犯的錯誤，應注意。）

Track 83

329

錯誤 The answer **of** the question is on page 10.

正確 The answer **to** the question is on page 10.

中譯 問題的答案在第十頁。

突破盲點!!

一般而言，一個問題的答案不「屬於」問題本身，故介系詞不可使用 of，應用 to，因為答案是要用來「去」回答問題的。同理 the solution of the problem 亦為錯誤，應改為 the solution to the problem。

330

錯誤 I am not very good **in** English.

正確 I am not very good **at** English.

中譯 我英文很不好。

突破盲點!!

「擅長……」英文通常用 be good at，而不用 be good in。

331

錯誤 What did the manager **say** you?

正確 1. What did the manager **say to** you?

正確 2. What did the manager **tell** you?

中譯 1. 經理跟你說了什麼？
2. 經理告訴了你什麼？

突破盲點!!

Say 不可直接用「人」當受詞，必須加介系詞 to，但 tell 可直接以「人」為受詞。

332

錯誤 What did you **tell to** her?

正確 What did you **tell** her?

中譯 你告訴了她什麼？

突破盲點!!

Tell 可用「人」當受詞，不須加介系詞 to。注意，勿將 tell 的用法與 say 的用法混淆，後者不可直接以「人」作受詞，須先加介系詞 to，如：What did you say to her?

Track 84

333

A: Thank you very much.

錯誤	B: Don't **mention about** it.
正確	B: Don't **mention** it.

中譯　A：非常謝謝你。
B：不用客氣。

突破盲點!!

Mention 為及物動詞，其後不須加介系詞，直接跟受詞。

NOTES

7

疑問句
Questions

A. 直接和間接問句 Direct and Indirect Questions

B. 其他問句 Other Questions

A. 直接和間接問句 Direct and Indirect Questions

334

錯誤 **How to** spell it?

正確 **How do you** spell it?

中譯 這個怎麼拼寫？

突破盲點!!

不論何種句型，英文的句子一定要有主詞和動詞。本句為疑問句，因此還得加助動詞 do，句子才算完整。

335

錯誤 **How to** pronounce this word?

正確 **How do you** pronounce this word?

中譯 這個字怎麼唸？

突破盲點!!

很顯然，錯誤的句子是由中文直接翻譯過去的。英文文法較中文嚴謹，一個句子一定要有主詞和動詞，本句子為疑問句，因此還得加助動詞 do。

Track 85

336 錯誤 **How to** say that in Chinese?

正確 **How do you say** that in Chinese?

中譯 那個中文怎麼說？

突破盲點!!

受中文直譯的影響，錯誤的句子在英文中並不是完整的句子。英文句子一定要有主詞和動詞。另外，由於本句為疑問句，故須加助動詞 do。

337 錯誤 How **it can** be used?

正確 How **can it** be used?

中譯 這個要怎麼用呢？

突破盲點!!

本句為以疑問副詞 how 所引導的疑問句，句中之主詞 it 應與助動詞 can 對調，形成倒裝句型。

338 錯誤 Can you tell me where **can** I find a restroom?

正確 Can you tell me where I **can** find a restroom?

中譯 你可以告訴我在哪可以找到廁所嗎？

突破盲點!!

Where can I find a restroom? 為一直接問句，故本句中之 where 子句為 tell 的受詞，故主詞與動詞的位置要還原，即，改成一間接問句（名詞子句）以作為動詞 tell 之受詞。

B. 其他問句 Other Questions

339 錯誤 **Are you come** to visit our factory?

正確 1. **Are you coming** to visit our factory?

正確 2. **Will you come** to visit our factory?

中譯 1. 你要來參觀我們的工廠嗎？ 2. 你會來參觀我們的工廠嗎？

突破盲點!!

Come 為一般動詞（不及物），如與 be 動詞連用，應出現進行式。注意，本句的現在進行式用來表示「未來」，故本句亦可直接用未來式。

Track 86

340

錯誤 **Are you study** Chinese?

正確 1. **Do you study** Chinese?

正確 2. **Are you studying** Chinese now?

中譯 1. 你學中文嗎？

2. 你現在在學中文嗎？

突破盲點!!

Study 為普通動詞，使用在疑問句時，須加助動詞 do，或加 be 動詞，再使用現在分詞，構成進行式。

341

錯誤 **Do** you still thirsty?

正確 **Are** you still thirsty?

中譯 你口還渴嗎？

突破盲點!!

Thirsty 是一個形容詞，不是動詞，因此句中需要動詞（而非助動詞）。本句中的動詞 are 是 be 動詞，主詞是 you，而 thirsty 則是主詞補語。

342 錯誤 **Do** you **like** to attend the year-end party this weekend?

正確 1. **Do** you **want** to attend the year-end party this weekend?

正確 2. **Would** you **like** to attend the year-end party this weekend?

中譯 1. 你想參加這個週末的年終派對嗎？
2. 你要不要來參加這個週末的年終派對？

突破盲點!!

Like 一般作「喜歡」解，如：Do you like English?；如作「想要」解時，應與助動詞 would（表「客氣」）連用，否則應直接用 want。

343 錯誤 Would you like **watching** a movie tonight?

正確 Would you like **to watch** a movie tonight?

中譯 你今天晚上想看電影嗎？

突破盲點!!

在 Would you like 之後一定要用不定詞 (to V)，不可用動名詞 (Ving)。注意，勿將 Would you like 和 Would you mind 搞混；於後者之後應接動名詞，如：Would you mind opening the window?。

Track 87

344

錯誤 What **we can** do if they withdraw their offer?

正確 What **can we** do if they withdraw their offer?

中譯 如果他們撤回他們原來出的價錢我們該怎麼辦？

突破盲點!!

本句為疑問句，故須將主詞 we 與助動詞 can「倒裝」，即將 can 置於 we 之前。

345

錯誤 What is the difference **of** your old product and your new product?

正確 What is the difference **between** your old product and your new product?

中譯 你們的舊產品和新產品有什麼不同？

突破盲點!!

本句問的是新產品與舊產品「之間」有何不同，正確的介系詞應為 between。

346 錯誤

If there is a problem with the computer system, **how** should I do?

正確

If there is a problem with the computer system, **what** should I do?

中譯　如果電腦系統有問題，我該怎麼辦？

突破盲點!!

「我該怎麼辦？」應該說成 What should I do?；how 為一疑問副詞，指的是「如何（做一件事）」，如：How should I do it?。

347 錯誤

How do you think about our offer?

正確

What do you think about our offer?

中譯　你覺得我們的出價如何？

突破盲點!!

How 為疑問副詞，應用來修飾動詞；本句並非問「如何想」，故不能使用 how。What do you think? 就是「你意下如何？」、「你覺得怎樣？」的意思。

Track 88

348

A: Hi, Bill!

錯誤	B: Oh, hi, Allen. **How about** your weekend?
正確	B: Oh, hi, Allen. **How was** your weekend?

中譯　A：嗨！比爾。
B：嗨！艾倫。你週末過得如何？

突破盲點!!

How about ... 用來問人對某事的「意見」，如：How about some beer?

NOTES

8

其他錯誤
Other Errors

A. 否定表達 Negatives / Negation

B. 話語標記 Discourse Markers

C. 時間表達 Time

D. 文字順序 Word Order (Inversions)

A. 否定表達 Negatives / Negation

349

錯誤 I drink neither coffee **or** tea.

正確 I drink neither coffee **nor** tea.

中譯 我不喝咖啡也不喝茶。

突破盲點!!

Neither 之後一定跟 nor，而 either 之後一定跟 or，不可任意變更。

350

錯誤 I **can not** hardly wait to meet them.

正確 I **can** hardly wait to meet them.

中譯 我迫不及待想與他們見面。

突破盲點!!

Hardly 是「幾乎不」，它本身就包含「否定」的意思，因此不可再加否定詞 not。

Track 89

351

A: I don't think I'll go to the meeting tomorrow.

錯誤 B: I don't think I'll go, **too**.

正確 B: I don't think I'll go, **either**.

中譯 A：我想我明天不會去開會。
B：我想我也不會去。

突破盲點!!

表示「否定」的「也」，應該用 either；too 只能表「肯定」的「也」，如：A: I think I'll go. B: I think I'll go, too.

352

錯誤 It **sounds not** good.

正確 It **doesn't sound** good.

中譯 聽起來不是很好。

突破盲點!!

Sound 為一普通動詞，表否定須藉助於助動詞。

B. 話語標記 Discourse Markers

353 錯誤

We cannot accept your offer for two reasons. First, the price is just too high. **Besides**, the color selection is not broad enough.

正確

We cannot accept your offer for two reasons. First, the price is just too high. **Besides that**, the color selection is not broad enough.

中譯 我們不能接受你們的出價有兩個原因。首先，價錢實在太高。除此之外，顏色的選擇也不夠多。

突破盲點!!

本例中由於第一句明白指出有「兩」個原因，故「除第一個原因之外」應用 besides that 表達。注意 besides 的這個用法為介系詞，如單獨使用 besides「而且」，則為副詞，意思不夠清楚。

Track 90

354 錯誤 **Although** sales have declined recently, **but** we want to invest in the new project.

正確 1. **Although** sales have declined recently, we want to invest in the new project.

正確 2. Sales have declined recently, **but** we want to invest in the new project.

中譯 1. 雖然最近業務下滑，可是我們還是想投資這項新的專案。
2. 最近業務下滑，但我們還是想投資這項新的專案。

突破盲點!!

Although 為從屬連接詞，but 為對等連接詞，二者不可同時使用（雖然中文可以說「雖然……，但是……」），只能擇一。

355 錯誤 **Since** the new product is very successful, **so** we want to celebrate.

正確 1. **Since** the new product is very successful, we want to celebrate.

正確 2. The new product is very successful, **so** we want to celebrate.

中譯 1. 因為新產品非常成功，我們想慶祝一番。
2. 新產品非常成功，所以我們想慶祝一番。

突破盲點!!

Since（或 because）為從屬連接詞，so 為對等連接詞，二者不可同時使用（雖然中文說「因為……，所以……」），須擇一。

356 錯誤 **At last**, I want to talk about financing.

正確 **Last/Finally**, I want to talk about financing.

中譯 最後，我想談談財務問題。

突破盲點!!

At last 是「終於」的意思，不適用於本句，應改為 Last 或 Finally「最後」。

Track 91

357

A: I'm going to get a cup of coffee before going to the conference room.

錯誤	B: I'll go find the room **at first** and then go to the restroom.
正確	B: I'll go find the room **first** and then go to the restroom.

中譯 A：我去會議室之前要先弄杯咖啡喝。
B：我會先找到會議室然後去上個洗手間。

突破盲點!!

At first 是「最初、開始時」的意思，與句意不符，應直接用副詞 first，表示「首先」。

358 錯誤 **As** I know, the budget does not include travel expenses.

正確 **As far as** I know, the budget does not include travel expenses.

中譯 就我所知，預算不包含旅遊費用。

突破盲點!!

As I know 文法上雖不算錯，但在句中並無特別意義（如改為 As you know，則有提醒對方的功能），應改成 As far as I know。

C. 時間表達 Time

359 錯誤 I left the advertising agency **for two years**.

正確 I left the advertising agency **two years ago**.

中譯 我兩年前就離開廣告公司了。

突破盲點!!

本句動詞為過去式，但時間卻是 for two years（表示到現在已經兩年）不合理，應改為 two years ago。

Track 92

360 錯誤 I receive the Italian orders **one week two times**.

正確 I receive the Italian orders **two times/twice a week**.

中譯 我一個星期收到兩次義大利的訂單。

突破盲點!!

「一星期兩次」應該說 (two times/twice a week)，英文沒有 one week two times 的說法。

361 錯誤 You are **older than me five years**.

正確 You are **five years older than me**.

中譯 你比我大五歲。

突破盲點!!

在英文比較的結構中，若要表示「數目」的差異，必須置於比較級之前。

362 錯誤 The **last time when** we attended the trade show, we took a lot of orders.

正確 The **last time** we attended the trade show, we took a lot of orders.

中譯　我們上次參加貿易展接到很多訂單。

突破盲點!!

原句中的關係副詞 when 表「時間」，而它的先行詞本來就是時間 (time)，故常將 when 省略。類似常見的另一個例子是 the reason (why) ...。

363 錯誤 Sometimes I get up **at midnight** to have a glass of milk.

正確 Sometimes I get up **in the middle of the night** to have a glass of milk.

中譯　我有時候會半夜起來喝一杯牛奶。

突破盲點!!

At midnight 指「在午夜 (12：00) 的時候」；in the middle of the night 才是中文說的「半夜」。

Track 93

364

錯誤 The last time I saw her was ten years **before**.

正確 The last time I saw her was ten years **ago**.

中譯 我上次看到她是十年前的事。

突破盲點!!

以「現在時間」為基點的「以前」要用 ago；before 則用在以「過去時間」為基點的「以前」，如：five days before he was killed「他遇害五天前」。

365

錯誤 **What time** will the exhibition be held next year?

正確 **When** will the exhibition be held next year?

中譯 明年的展覽什麼時候會舉辦？

突破盲點!!

What time 問的是「時刻」即「幾點鐘」，依句意本句問的應是 when「什麼時候」；但 when 有時可取代 what time，即 when 也可用來問「時刻」。

366

錯誤 I will arrive ten minutes **later**.

正確 I will arrive **in** ten minutes.

中譯 我會在十分鐘後到達。

突破盲點!!

Later 前若加「一段時間」指「在另一先前提到的時間之後」，因此通常用在講過去之事；以「現在」為基準時之「之後」則應用 in 再加「一段時間」。

D. 文字順序 Word Order (Inversions)

367

錯誤 Here **Joe comes**!

正確 Here **comes Joe**!

中譯 喬來了！

突破盲點!!

以 here 或 there 起頭，用來引起對某人或某物的注意之句子，須採「倒裝」形式，即，將主詞與動詞對調位置（如本句，或 There goes Joe!）。但若主詞為人稱代名詞時，則不須倒裝，如 Here he comes! 或 There he goes!。

Track 94

368 錯誤 The conference center is **eastsouth** of the city.

正確 The conference center is **southeast** of the city.

中譯 會議中心在城市的東南方。

「東南」乃中文之說法，英文應倒過來說：southeast，直譯即為「南東」；同理「西北」則為 northwest。

369 錯誤 You can find the answer on the **left lower** corner of the page.

正確 You can find the answer on the **lower left** corner of the page.

中譯 你可以在頁面的左下角找到答案。

突破盲點!!

「左下角」為中文的說法，英文的表達方式為 lower left corner（直譯即為「下左角」）；同理「右上角」應說成 upper right corner。

370

A: Did you put your personal data on the form?

錯誤 B: Yes, I **filled in it** completely.

正確 B: Yes, I **filled it in** completely.

中譯 A：你把個人資料都填入表格裡了嗎？
B：是的，我全都填入了。

突破盲點!!

Fill in 是「填寫」的意思，為一雙字動詞（two-word verb），若其受詞為代名詞時，必須放在 fill 與 in 之間。其他相同的例子包括：call him up、look it up、turn it over……等等。

371

錯誤 If my computer stops working again, I will **take apart it** myself.

正確 If my computer stops working again, I will **take it apart** myself.

中譯 如果我的電腦又當機，我會自己把它拆了。

突破盲點!!

Take apart 為一雙字動詞 (two-word verb)，若其受詞為代名詞須置於 take 與 apart 之間，不可放在後面。

Track 95

372 錯誤

The number we will buy depends on how expensive **is their product**.

正確

The number we will buy depends on how expensive **their product is**.

中譯　我們會買多少得看他們的產品有多貴。

突破盲點!!

Depend on 後須接受詞，其後若為一問句，須改為間接問句（即名詞子句），換言之，主詞 their product 與動詞 is 須倒裝。

373 錯誤

Are you the **responsible person** for overseas orders?

正確

Are you the **person responsible** for overseas orders?

中譯　你是負責海外訂貨的人嗎？

突破盲點!!

Responsible 直接修飾名詞時，意思是「負責任的」；responsible for 則指「為……負責」。

374 錯誤 Let me tell you **two my** ideas.

正確 Let me tell you **my two** ideas.

中譯 讓我告訴你我的兩個想法。

英文中若有所有形容詞和數字形容詞修飾同一個名詞，所有格須在前，數字在後。(本句亦可將數字 two 作代名詞，置於 my 之前，但須加介系詞 of，如：two of my ideas。

國家圖書館出版品預行編目資料

正確出口說英文 / Dana Forsythe 作；-- 初版. -- 臺北市：
貝塔, 2015. 07
面； 公分
ISBN: 978-986-92044-0-8（平裝附光碟片）
1. 英語 2. 語法

805.16 104012341

正確出口說英文

作　　者 / Dana Forsythe
執行編輯 / 朱慧瑛

出　　版 / 貝塔出版有限公司
地　　址 / 台北市 100 館前路 12 號 11 樓
電　　話 / (02) 2314-2525
傳　　真 / (02) 2312-3535
郵　　撥 / 19493777 貝塔出版有限公司
客服專線 / (02) 2314-3535
客服信箱 / btservice@betamedia.com.tw

總 經 銷 / 時報文化出版企業股份有限公司
地　　址 / 桃園市龜山區萬壽路二段 351 號
電　　話 / (02) 2306-6842

出版日期 / 2015 年 9 月初版一刷
定　　價 / 320 元
海外定價 / 美金 14 元
I S B N / 978-986-92044-0-8

貝塔網址：www.betamedia.com.tw

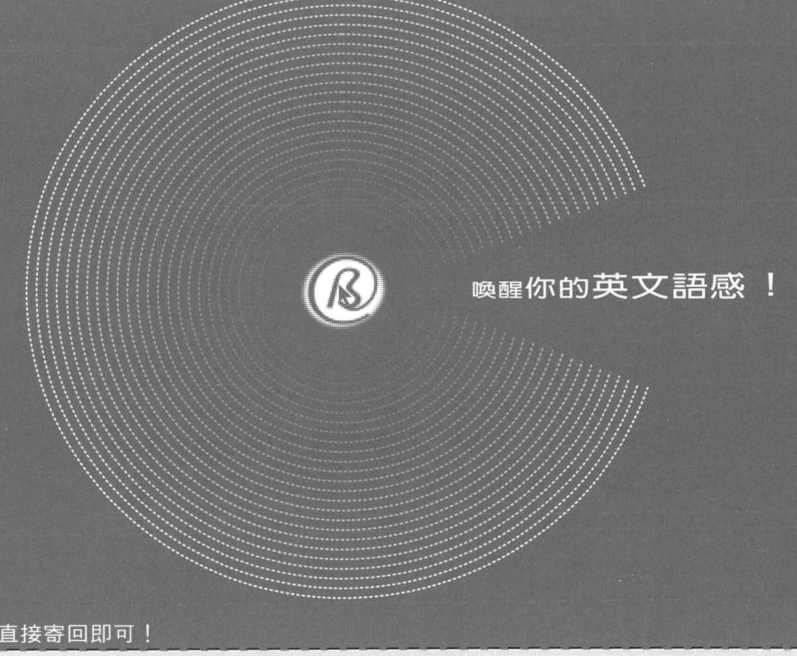

請對折後釘好，直接寄回即可！

廣 告 回 信
北區郵政管理局登記證 北台字第14256號
免 貼 郵 票

100 台北市中正區館前路12號11樓

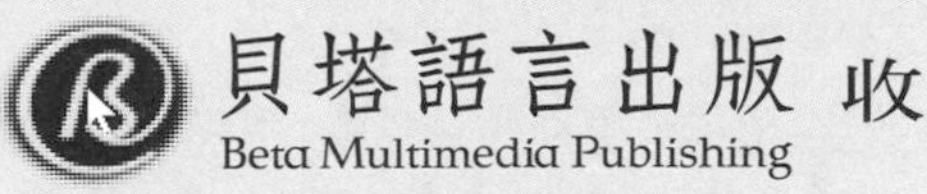

寄件者住址 □□□

讀者服務專線（02）2314-3535　讀者服務傳真（02）2312-3535
客戶服務信箱 btservice@betamedia.com.tw
www.betamedia.com.tw

謝謝您購買本書！！

貝塔語言擁有最優良之英文學習書籍，為提供您最佳的英語學習資訊，您可填妥此表後寄回（免貼郵票）將可不定期收到本公司最新發行書訊及活動訊息！

姓名：＿＿＿＿＿＿＿＿＿＿ 性別：□男 □女 生日：＿＿＿年＿＿＿月＿＿＿日

電話：(公)＿＿＿＿＿＿＿＿＿(宅)＿＿＿＿＿＿＿＿＿(手機)＿＿＿＿＿＿＿＿

電子信箱：＿＿＿＿＿＿＿＿＿＿＿＿＿＿＿＿＿＿＿＿

學歷：□高中職含以下 □專科 □大學 □研究所含以上

職業：□金融 □服務 □傳播 □製造 □資訊 □軍公教 □出版

□自由 □教育 □學生 □其他

職級：□企業負責人 □高階主管 □中階主管 □職員 □專業人士

1．您購買的書籍是？＿＿＿＿＿＿＿＿＿＿＿＿＿＿＿＿

2．您從何處得知本產品？(可複選)

□書店 □網路 □書展 □校園活動 □廣告信函 □他人推薦 □新聞報導 □其他

3．您覺得本產品價格：

□偏高 □合理 □偏低

4．請問目前您每週花了多少時間學英語？

□ 不到十分鐘 □ 十分鐘以上，但不到半小時 □ 半小時以上，但不到一小時

□ 一小時以上，但不到兩小時 □ 兩個小時以上 □ 不一定

5．通常在選擇語言學習書時，哪些因素是您會考慮的？

□ 封面 □ 內容、實用性 □ 品牌 □ 媒體、朋友推薦 □ 價格□ 其他＿＿＿＿＿

6．市面上您最需要的語言書種類為？

□ 聽力 □ 閱讀 □ 文法 □ 口說 □ 寫作 □ 其他＿＿＿＿＿＿

7．通常您會透過何種方式選購語言學習書籍？

□ 書店門市 □ 網路書店 □ 郵購 □ 直接找出版社 □ 學校或公司團購

□ 其他＿＿＿＿＿＿＿

8．給我們的建議：＿＿＿＿＿＿＿＿＿＿＿＿＿＿＿＿＿＿＿＿＿＿＿＿＿＿＿＿＿＿

＿＿＿＿＿＿＿＿＿＿＿＿＿＿＿＿＿＿＿＿＿＿＿＿＿＿＿＿＿＿＿＿＿＿＿＿＿＿

喚醒你的英文語感！

Get a Feel for English !